A BURIAL IN MY BACKYARD

HITESH TREHON

Published By :
Aksharansh Publication
An imprint of kharidobecho.in
Hinjewadi Phase - 3, Pune (M.H.) - 411057
Tel : (020) - 41243975, Mo : +91-7380434014

ISBN : **978-93-92445-79-8**

Processed & printed in India

Earlier Books by Author

Dedication

*This book is dedicated to thousands of **innocent men and women** languishing in various jails in the country for many years awaiting justice. Whether there's not enough proof or if the police make up a big case with fake reports, often involving money changing hands, the real criminal gets away, and someone innocent, usually poor, has to suffer the consequences.*

Sadly human life has no value or respect.

Chapter One

I was the sixth sibling of three brothers and two sisters - an unwanted result of a surprised pregnancy of my mother in her mid-forties.

No one cared about me, how I learned, or what I achieved in life. My own determination and of course the love and affection of my grandparents as a new toy for their life, indifferent to all at home, encouraged me to be an accounting graduate from an 'A' grade college which fetched me a reasonably good job.

Our house was a big bungalow built by my grandpa and was situated at Juhu, a suburb of Mumbai close to a renowned famous film director and producer.

As time went by, my three brothers Mahinder, Manoj and Mohan married and drifted away. My two sisters Sharda and Mona were too married into good families and settled in Delhi.

My father worked at a Bank and was transferred to the Chennai branch that also had their head office in the same city and because he was on promotion, he had to stay there until retirement.

The joy in my grandparents was evident when the house had only three residents, with just me being present.

My grandpa Satyadev Batra had three refit service showrooms; selling and fitting expensive accessories for high end cars and SUVs at Santa Cruz, Khar, and at Bandra. He was content, running a business that provided more than enough to support his dependents until they moved to other cities.

Early morning the three of us would go over to Juhu beach and walk for 45 minutes and return home.

While the breakfast was being readied by my grandmother, I would take a shower and be ready for work. Same was my grandpa's routine.

After breakfast, I would sit in the Maruti 800 and be dropped at Santacruz station and with a cheerful goodbye my grandpa would leave for his shop.

In a matter of moments, I would find myself enveloped and encircled by fellow passengers within the bustling suburban compartment. Bodies pressed against one another, a sea of humanity, with the electric train gracefully swaying on its tracks at high speed, creating a symphony of movement and connection.

One fine day, after a walk on the beach, when I came down for breakfast I was surprised to see that grandpa was not dressed for work.

'Not feeling well grandpa?' I asked with a little concern.

'Nothing like that puttar (son, in Punjabi) I've shut the shops for good. Your grandma is getting old and frail and we decided to quit business. I have saved enough to carry on until we are no more.' I made a shattered face and turned to leave.

'If you want you can run the shops.'

'No Dadaji, I'm unfit for such things. Let the shops stay shut or else you may lease them or sell all the spare parts and later sell the shops.'

Saying so, I left for work, however the routine was altered by my taking a bus to the station and then boarding a train.

In a few months, my grandma didn't wake up in the morning. She passed away peacefully without even disturbing her husband who slept by her side. The cremation was carried out by my dadaji and myself in the presence of a few neighbours.

At the age of 25, I was a tall, fair, and handsome looking Punjabi youth. I had sharp features with thick growth of black hair combed with a thin parting on the left. My features were magnificent and manly like a Royal lion gauging at various animals in the prairie and finally selecting a prey to devour. A lion is fierce but I have a docile and trustworthy demeanour. I love women and women love and trust me.

My daily walks on the beach were reduced from a full week to 3 days. Either grandpa was not present or I had late nights with sexy damsels.

Chapter Two

With days passing by, and then years vanishing, my grandpa got really sick. I hired a male attendant to look after his needs and be a companion to him while I was away. The attendant cost me half of my salary but there was no way out. I cut down on McDonald's lunch and shifted to cheap Udupi thali. I also cut down on the occasional luxury of hiring a cab to the office from the railway station.

On Sundays, I would drive him to Juhu beach and make him sit on a plastic chair and I could see the happiness on his face. I actually loved him from the days of my childhood. He would tell me beautiful stories and buy me anything I wanted.

One fine day grandpa requested me to take leave from my work.

'It's important and I don't have much time left.' So quickly, I phoned my office.

'Take me to Mr. Seth's office.' We sat in his car and headed for Vile Parle West, a lane behind Nanavati Hospital.

This was the first time that I had entered the office of dadaji's advocate.

With my support we trudged into a spacious office.

'Seth saab have you got all the papers ready?' My grandpa said as he saw Mr. Seth.

'Yes sir, everything is ready and I have also arranged for the cameraman to be present.'

'So let's start! Why waste time?' Seth asked my grandpa and requested him to talk about his will.

'I, Satyadev Batra, in full presence of mind, sign my last will gifting all that I own by way of properties, cash, shares and stocks and my house as enumerated in my Will to my grandson Mahavir Batra who is presently standing by my side and whom I love very much. Nobody other than my grandson is entitled to all that is mentioned in my will.' The will is put in front of grandpa and myself and accordingly we both sign which is recorded on camera along with the two retired judges signing as witnesses and our family doctor issuing a certificate mentioning my grandpa in good frame of mind to sign the Will.

A while later, we enter the registrar's office and have the will attested.

The registrar is well looked after by Mr. Seth.

'Dadaji you are going to live a long life, why the hurry?'

'Sonny, when death is calling, all that is materialistic is of no use but it is important to diligently get rid of it by bequeathing to the right person and my child you have always been by my side and your grandma held you in high regards. I am confident that you are the right person.' He lifts his hand and caresses my cheek.

Within days, my grandpa took his last breath in my arms. Despite having a large family, I was left alone.

All family members came for the funeral and after the 4th day of cremation (Chautha) we all sat on the sofas i.e. my mom and dad, and my three brothers. My two sisters did not attend the funeral. All of them looked at one another as if asking the question about who will initiate the matter of the will. All eyes were directed at my father who then took the lead.

'I will call your grandfather's advocate Mr. Seth to our residence over here and discuss his Will and inheritance. All to be present, no running away for shopping or meeting your friends.' All of them shook their heads in affirmation like dummies and then quietly dispersed.

I wonder why we didn't sit and talk and maybe have food together and indulge as a family ?"

"It's a sad sad world we live in Master Jack." Suddenly, this song reminded me of my loneliness and the sadness this world holds.

I went to my room and returned with a bottle of Royal Challenge, poured myself a three finger slug and added the same quantity of water and took a big gulp with a satisfying sigh. Others looked aghast and my dad was first to speak, by now the whiskey had entered my adrenaline.

'How dare you drink in front of me without taking my permission, I'm your dad!'He raised his voice.

'Oh really? When was the last time you spoke to me? Eight years ago?" I scoffed and then I gulped more whiskey. In a matter of time, my other brothers went to the bar and poured themselves a respectable peg.

'Dad come and join us, it's a reunion of our family.' my eldest brother Mahinder sourly pleaded.

The drinking seemed weird, like four men meeting on a train and each trying to know about the other. By the time the last drop was squeezed out of the bottle all had some idea about what each of us did for a living and they shamelessly heard how our grandparents passed away.

Food was ordered from a restaurant, consumed, and the table was left with dishes scattered. Each person then headed cautiously to their bedrooms.

'Tomorrow is an important day.' My eldest brother slurred and shut his door.

The next morning, the table was laid and a steel tray with fried eggs, chicken sausages, fried potatoes and a kettle of hot coffee was meticulously laid on the table. There goes my monthly ration. I felt miserable.

It seemed all had timed it behind my back to meet at the breakfast table at 9:00 AM sharp.

'Saab, I'm leaving the job if I have to cook for so many people, I cannot handle it!'

My typical Maharashtrian maid, cook, housekeeping and once in a while romping partner declared in front of my hungry family.

'Kantabai, please bear with me until tomorrow, they all are leaving tomorrow.' I said loudly so all could hear.

'How have you decided that we are leaving tomorrow, this is OUR house!' My father shouted. I stayed quiet, in two hours all of them will know.

At sharp 11:00 AM, advocate Seth was escorted in and he chose to sit on a straight chair. He was accompanied by a photographer who set up a tripod and placed a movie camera ready to record the proceedings, except myself, all others were confused and silently observed as Advocate prepared to address all who were present.

Seth explained to all that the Will was prepared when Batra saab was sane in his mind and in the presence of a doctor and all that was wished were recorded and had clearly mentioned that he was under no duress or compulsion from any member of his family to prepare the Will that has been signed and registered. Complete silence prevailed with faces showing expectations.

Seth ceremoniously opened his briefcase and pulled out the hard bound Will and started reading.

The first two paragraphs gave scathing remarks about the neglect meted out to him and his wife by his son and all his grandchildren except myself, his loving youngest grandson Mahavir. The rest of the Will created a pandemonium and shouting and threatening me that I orchestrated grandpa's Will to my advantage.

None of the family members bequeathed even a Rupee. Everything that was owned by my grandpa was now mine.

The family threatened to go to Court and I kept quiet as per the teachings of my late grandfather though I could threaten them all to leave the house by tomorrow morning or else I will file an FIR with the police department for trespassing my property.

The full lot of them left the house and most probably shifted to a hotel to get hold of a lawyer and contest the Will.

Who cares, I thought.

Chapter Three

I employed a Valuer to assess the wealth my grandpa left for me. Included in my assets are my current residence, fixed deposits, shares and stocks, as well as cash in both savings and current accounts. Additionally, I possess my grandma's jewellery securely stored in bank lockers, among other items.

After about 10 days Mr. Pandey the Valuer sat across from me. His face showed envy and blurted out a stupendous amount that I had inherited.

'Your grandfather had been buying properties since 1980. For instance, he purchased an apartment on Cuffs Parade near Nariman Point for Rs. 1.8 Lacs and the value of the same in today's market is around Rs. 75 Crores which fetches him a handsome rental. When you go through the dossier, you will find many such properties.'

He handed over a fifty page spiral bound broad notebook which had comprehensive details and valuations of all my current possessions.

I was for sure a rich man! As I perused through this tangible account of my journey, I couldn't help but feel a profound sense of gratitude for the richness that life had bestowed upon me.

It took me two days of hard drinking and sex with some failed tv actor to return back on Earth and sober up. After absorbing the weight of my material wealth, I couldn't help but ponder the intangible treasures that the pages failed to capture— the memories, the experiences, and the invaluable moments that truly define the essence of ownership. In the tapestry of life, this notebook served as a map, guiding me through the tangible and intangible realms that together compose the mosaic of my existence.

1. I consider myself a discerning individual, understanding the distinction between leading a wasteful life and enjoying it in a healthy manner. Recognizing certain priorities that required my attention, I made the deliberate decision to start by resigning from my job.

2. Lock up all bedrooms on the upper floor. The ground floor was big enough for just me. It had two bedrooms, a large living hall and dining area with a square kitchen. The whole area looked desolate with faded paint on walls. I needed to uplift the vibes to make it pleasing for my existence, so I appointed an interior designer.

3. Miss Amita Bhatnagar was a famous designer in the Western suburbs. She entered my house like a lavender hue and agreed to do up the house. She probed into my personality, my likes and dislikes and having made her inner impression of me, she agreed to visit the following day with submission to changes in painting the walls, furnishing the living hall and rest of the ground floor. I need to mention here that I would stutter

whenever I spoke to her because I was baffled by the sheer beauty of this young lady. She had a lovely set of teeth wherein the front four teeth were slightly long and milky white. I would give my life to place my nose close to her mouth and smell the fragrance that she emitted from her pouty lips. She wore an off white saree with small imprinted rose buds with a matching blouse and her saree pallu covered her front but soon my eyes were able to penetrate her shield and realised that she was endowed with well formed breasts. My loins stirred.

4. Within four weeks the interior walls were painted, all old furniture was discarded and replaced with exquisite furnishing to my liking. The kitchen was now fitted with the latest gadgets, including a combo oven and Faber brand Exhaust system.

5. The outer surface of the bungalow was pleasingly painted with the boundary wall re-plastered with automated opening of the gate and having a small room built for the security guard.

6. The front had a parking space for three cars and my grandpa's old car looked like a sore thumb. I sold it for scrap and purchased a glistening limousine and a masculine SUV. The exchange marked not just a shift in my transportation but also a symbol of embracing opulence and versatility on my journey forward.

7. Finally, I tackled the large area at the back of the bungalow which showed signs of being a beautiful and large

backyard garden probably well curated by my late grandma during her younger days. I got hold of a contractor and got the garden back in shape with a lot of saplings grown and with ready made patches of Mexican grass slapped onto the red barren ground. Under the skilled hands of the contractor, the garden blossomed into a sanctuary of colour and texture. With each sapling rooted and every patch of Mexican grass adding its vibrant hue, the once neglected space now stood as a testament to the power of renewal and deliberate cultivation.

By the time I completed the above task, the monsoon had set in. I must also mention that all the expenditures that I did on the house, didn't make the slightest dent on my inheritance pocket. The house looked magnificent and liveable.

Miss Amita Bhatnagar handed me a thick envelope as we sat on the sofa, her shoulder length hair partly covered her face and I felt the intense desire to use my hand to replace her hair back onto the shoulder and admire her chiseled, angular jawline tapering to a prominent round chin, as if on cue. She flicked her hair back and politely said,'The final invoice is on page one and all measurements follow on remaining pages along with all charges, please go through it and give me a call on mobile in case you need any clarification. On Monday morning, I will call you for my cheque.I want to thank you for having faith in me and awarding me this contract.'

She saw me watching her mouth while speaking and immediately pursed her lips, being conscious of my stare.

'Why postpone it until Monday? I'll settle your dues right away. No need for meticulous measurements; I'll take care of it now.' I rose to fetch my cheque book.

Having signed the cheque and handed it over, I said to her, 'Would you mind if I invite you to dinner tomorrow night to celebrate the successful completion of your assignment? It's not about being forward, but I genuinely want to express my appreciation and acknowledge your hard work over a nice dinner.'

'But I don't mix business with pleasure.'

'But who's asking for pleasure, I'm just requesting you to have dinner with me? Let us assume a dinner between a client and yourself.'

She was trapped with my sincere emphasis. She remained silent for a moment and said, 'I've never done this but nevertheless I consent to your invitation and would request a venue close to Khar suburban. Give me a call once you have decided the restaurant and time and please we will make it for early evening.'

Without casting a glance backward, she settled into her car and smoothly drove away. The fading tail lights marked the end of our encounter, leaving me with a moment of reflection on the unspoken connections that come and go in life's fleeting chapters.

I felt like going to her car, smashing the window glass of her car and planting a kiss on her fair cheeks. I saw my urge slipping away as her car whisked away from my sight.

Chapter Four

I sat alone thinking about nothing, later I stretched on my sofa and gradually drifted away. I dreamt of a weird dream of being engulfed within a high cubicle, having very tall concrete walls open to the sky having no exit and too high, it then rained and the level of water rising and being a good swimmer I lay floating on my back. The water kept on rising in the square cubicle and simultaneously my body rose accordingly until the level of water reached on top and started overflowing. I looked at the sky and then looked at the ground down below. It scared me because there was no way I could climb down except to jump from top and die due to the fall.

I woke up with a startle, my face dripping in perspiration, I tried to analyse the dream using Freud's theory of 'Interpretation of Dreams'. I concluded that my rising from a downtrodden man to being rich and staying rich needed me to streamline my life astutely. I felt my way in the dark and switched on the lights and went across to a window and heard the rain splashing on the ground, the first shower of the coming monsoon season.

The Meeting:

In the grandeur of The Marriott Hotel near the International Airport, I found myself immersed in the opulent surroundings, my gaze fixated on the entrance. Amidst the stream of elegantly poised women gracing the lobby, my anticipation found its culmination when Amita Bhatnagar appeared before me. Our eyes met, and she exuded a demure charm in a knee-length black lace frock, adorned with four-inch heels. Her shoulder-length hair cascaded freely, complementing the graceful contours of her makeup-free oval face, adorned only with a touch of eyeliner and a bold, shocking pink lipstick. In that moment, she had seamlessly transitioned from a diligent professional to a modern, sophisticated career woman, a transformation that held my undivided attention.

'Don't keep staring at me, it makes me uncomfortable and your stare is embarrassing me.' She commanded and I obeyed by looking in other directions.

We proceeded to the rooftop restaurant and were guided to a corner table overlooking the airport runway.

'what would you prefer for a drink?'

'I'd like a blueberry delight stirred with 30 ml Grey goose.' she looked up to the waiter and requested with a smile.

'I'll have a margarita.' I ordered, she raised her eyebrows and smiled.

'So what's your line of work or business?' She asked and I dreaded the question.

'Nothing, I was getting the house done and then seriously thinking about what to do in life.' She made a sad face as if wondering why she accepted this date.

'So where did you get such a lot of money to do up the house? I sincerely hope I'm not sitting across from a con man, though you don't look like one.' She made a move to stand up. I begged her to sit and listen, thankfully she obliged. In that instant, the atmosphere became charged with an unspoken tension, a palpable shift that set the stage for a conversation that would unravel the intricacies of our connection.

I then narrated my life story, from being an unwanted child, disliked by my other siblings and a callus interest meted by my parents. The utter love my grandparents had for me, their passing away and the inheritance I bequeathed.

None of us realised that we were nearing the end of our second drink. Margaritas have a quicker effect and I was mildly floating.

We ordered food and knowing that we have to endure 30 minutes, the silence between us was hurting me and so I asked her about her family life and work.

'My father is active in the Army and is on a posting and so is my elder brother who was recently married. After a honeymoon holiday, he is also away on a posting. Many times, we three ladies are the only ones occupying a large Govt. Bungalow as my father is a Brigadier. My sister-in-law is my best friend and we enjoy the rapport that all three of us have. During the day my work keeps me busy.'

Our table was adorned with delectable dishes, and with a shared sense of hunger, we eagerly indulged in the feast before us.

'So what do you intend to do in your life or are you planning to withhold the time and money that you have inherited, have you set any goals?'

She inquired before savouring a morsel of roast lamb, letting the flavours unfold in a culinary dance within her mouth.

After concluding our dinner, we strolled towards the exit. While anticipating the valet to retrieve her car, I addressed her,

'Can I ask you something? Suppose you were in my place, what would you do with your life? No need to answer now, take your time and let me know on mobile or we could have dinner again and talk on this.'

'Good night and will surely call you.'

'Good night Miss Bhatnagar!'

'Call me Amita.' saying so, she drove off.

I lay in bed, replaying the evening with Amita in my head. It was confirmed that she had not fallen head over heels in love with me, but she saw in me an interesting guy, someone she didn't want to let pass by as a mere acquaintance that would fade away with time. I wish I was like a super human having the power to captivate her, lift her black laced dress and have her.

I shook my head and rebuked myself for having such intrusive thoughts towards a girl I would like to fall in love with.

As the effects of the two, or perhaps three, margaritas began to take hold, I found myself succumbing to their influence. Before long, I slipped into a reverie of sweet dreams, gently guiding me into a serene and profound slumber. The gentle lull of the night embraced me, and the world of dreams unfolded its enchanting tapestry, carrying me away into a realm of tranquility.

I was woken up by the loud clattering of pots and utensils and soon realised that my maid Kantabai was in the kitchen. I had given her a spare key to the front door.

Frankly, there were no utensils to wash since last night I had dinner with Amita, maybe she wanted attention since I had been ignoring her for sometime after having met Amita.

'Kantabai *ek* cup coffee, please!' I shouted for her to hear and then went over to the bathroom to freshen up.

Kantabai set the mug and a few crackers on the bedside table. I gave a satisfied sigh and looked up at her who stood with a fist resting on her slender hips.

'Saab I'm sorry to say that I will be leaving the job as my husband is transferred to Vashi but you need not worry I will give a replacement. She is a nice hard working elderly lady. She will do the work exactly as I work except not that.' She gave a mischievous smile and left for the day.

Frankly, I was happy about it because I can try to be a good boy and become worthy of my new found love, though it was presently one sided, Amita had still to decide.

It was pathetic that I lived the life of the riches and didn't work for it.

Interwoven fingers I placed under my head on the pillow and looked up to the ceiling as if I could find some answers written up for me to see.

Staring and staring at the ceiling but no dice. I then decided to delve into my situation to find an answer to my predicament. What could I do to occupy myself?

Chapter Five

I sat across Amita, both at a loss of words. The garden restaurant at the Sea Horizon hotel in Juhu was exquisite. We had opted for Sun downer to enjoy the setting of sun, have a cocktail or two and dinner.

'I've been thinking about what kind of work you could indulge in, so here it is…'

I interrupted immediately, and said,

'Listen Amita, let me be frank, I'm a sane man and with time I will for sure work out my life but for now I want to say that I'm in love with you and would love to marry you and live a life with lots of kids.' My two strong cocktails helped me to be bold.

I could see that she was taken aback but did not threaten to leave, I was relieved.

'But how can I marry someone who is jobless?'

I stopped her and asked, 'Would you like to marry me, are you attracted to me, then with time I would ask you to declare whether you love me?'

'Amita, my journey has been marked by a challenging childhood, a turbulent adolescence, and, until a couple of months ago, a traumatic youth. Perhaps, in this chapter of my life, God has bestowed blessings for the karmas of my past.'

I gently cradled her palms within my own, a delicate connection forming. She didn't pull away as I intertwined my right fingers with her left, the warmth from my hand mingling with hers. A subtle shiver ran through her, prompting her to retract her hand.

'This is how far we can go, that is holding hands. You will now have to take it further by meeting my parents and putting forth your intentions to marry me. From there on I will take over all relevant matters.'

'But do you love me, at least you can answer me?' I insisted.

'Of course I love you or else why would I want you to meet my parents.' She smiled.

I took her hand and kissed her palm.

'My dad is coming home for a week in the last week of June, it's an official visit but then in the evenings he is in our custody.' She looked at me and smiled again.

Following our dinner, we descended the steps to the beach, relishing the sensation of cool sand beneath our bare feet as we strolled hand in hand. Our meandering walk occasionally brought our thighs in contact, and at a perfect moment, we shared a kiss. The irresistible connection between us left her unable to resist. Describing the sweet flavour and fragrance emanating from her beautiful mouth is beyond words.

I wondered how life takes a turn, from a desolate existence to a limitless joy. I looked up in the heavens above and thanked Shiva, my God.

By the time I reached home, it had started drizzling, the sweet smell of Mother Earth filled my nostrils. I parked the car in the patio and walked up the front steps of the porch and entered the warmth of my home.

A couple of days later Amita phoned me, 'Listen Mahavir! I've been invited to a party and I want you to come. Various socialites from various streams of businesses will be present and quite possibly you may meet somebody who may give an idea or two on the kind of business you could take up. Secondly you will get access to other such parties and thus increase your social base. Frankly I seldom attend social gatherings but I sort of thought that it may help you.' I looked at my mobile and looked up in the sky and wondered why the whole world is hell bent to help me out.

'Sure love, I'll pick you up, just message me your google address.'

I picked her up from the gate of the Army Cantonment at Colaba and drove to Whirlwind housing society at Cuffe Parade. The lift zoomed up to 34th storey and the escalator opened straight into a melee of voices in the large living hall of the host. 'Jesus Christ! and I thought that I was rich.' I mumbled.

A towering figure, possibly two inches taller than my 6ft frame, approached. He gracefully bent halfway from his waist, planting a firm kiss on Amita's right cheek. With a gentle hold on her shoulders, he expressed, 'Thanks for coming, Amita, darling. You look absolutely gorgeous. And who is this handsome man chaperoning you?'

'He is Mahavir, a very dear friend. Let me introduce you to Sailesh, the host.' We exchanged handshakes, and Sailesh extended a warm welcome.

There were around 60-70 guests in a hall that could accommodate 150 guests.

'You are now on your own, go and mix with guests and I'll keep coming to you from time to time but watch out don't you fall for one of these females, I'm your girl, please remember that.' She earnestly scanned my face for my reaction.

'I love you!' I assured her and headed towards the bar.

It took me ten minutes to finally have a stiff whiskey in my hand. I took a big gulp to gain my self confidence and then I moved around barging into groups of four or five seriously discussing Stock Exchange, manufacturing trends, then into another group talking politics and then more groups discussing their planned holidays to Europe or some other interesting destinations. Always approached with polite curiosity by someone in the group, I would introduce myself as a friend of the host, and thus, seamlessly became a welcomed participant in their conversation.

The first drink had brought me in a melancholy mood and also more confidence in my presence. I freely spoke to men and women alike, drinks always made me look like a sexy man but today I refrained from indulging in flirting.

I loved Amita who had brought me here. I made my way to the open terrace. The full moon stared at me, I saw the huge silver coin slowly inching towards the edge of the ocean, it mesmerised me and I was determined to see the moon slowly dip into the horizon disappearing to rise another day.

'It does look like a huge coin, don't you think so?' A fine lady in black party dress came and stood next to me and joined me in quietly admiring the setting of the moon.

When the moon had set, she turned toward me and extended her hand and said,

'Hi, I'm Paro and I'm married. It gave me a nice feeling standing by your side.'

'You are beautiful, there are hardly any lights but your glow is now visible after the moon is set. I am not drunk but I never shy away from appreciating anything that deserves it. My name is Mahavir and I live in Juhu,' I observed that behind her smiling demeanour, she seemed to be a very sad woman.

'We also stay in Juhu, at Ruia Park, that's the other end of Juhu.'

'May I get you a drink?'

'No, I do not drink alcohol, I'll wait for my husband to have dinner, once he is finished with drinks.'

'Ah, here you are Paro, I was wondering where you were!'

'Meet Mr. Mahavir, he also lives in Juhu.' Paro introduced me.

'Where in Juhu? By the way, I'm Mukesh.' Paro's husband introduced himself..

'I stay close to the main beach, my bungalow is in front of the house of the famous film director V R Chabria.

"Oh, I'm familiar with your house. I've attended a few gatherings there, and I couldn't help but notice your previously neglected and forlorn-looking house across the street. Recently, though, it seems to have undergone a transformation with a fresh coat of paint, presenting a much more inviting appearance."

'Do you stay close by?'

'No, I stay near Ruia Park and pass your house daily while going to my office.'

'Well my grandparents were too old to look after the house, now that they are no longer alive I have refurbished the house.'

'So you live with your wife in the big house?'

'No, I live alone. I'm getting organised and once I get married to my girlfriend Amita, then it would be fine.'

'You have a lovely garden at the back, I used to admire it whenever the Chabrias invited me for a party. I hope you do justice to the garden and look after it.'

'Oh yes I have a full time gardener.' I chipped in.

'Mukesh, let's have dinner,' insisted the pleasant lady, encouraging her husband to join for the evening meal.

'Let's capture a moment, shall we? How about starting with a selfie?'

We gathered in unison, capturing the camaraderie in a series of delightful selfies that would serve as cherished mementos of our time together.

'Mahavir now you take a few, in case mine are not up to the mark then at least we have yours.' He then called a waiter to have the photos taken.

'Come closer to me Mukesh, why are you standing apart, let me get closer to Mahavir so we all can fit in this close up photo.' Mukesh hardly moved and the photograph was clicked.

'Let's be good friends and meet up soon.' Mukesh and Paro headed for dinner and I headed towards the bar.

As I sipped my 3rd peg, Amita came over and held me at the waist and said.

'Are you enjoying the party?'

'Yes it's great and I met some interesting people, are you hungry, we can eat if you want?'

'No it's Ok, we'll wait for sometime,' and Amita walked away from me.

The effects of the three substantial pegs began to take hold, plunging me deeper into a sense of melancholy. The lone guitarist, with a small amplifier, serenaded the surroundings with old love songs through the microphone on a stand, intensifying the nostalgic atmosphere.

I went over to him and offered to sing a song, I heard claps all around and having silenced the crowd with the actions of my hand I requested a lady volunteer to sing a duet from Raj Kapoor's film Awara.

'I know the song and I'll sing with you.' The guitarist tuned in and we sang. The song was well sung and at the end I put my left hand ever so softly on her shoulder and thanked her. I asked her name and she spoke in a husky voice and said 'Gayatri' photographs were clicked and the applause resonated in the big hall.

En route to her residence in Colaba, Amita matter-of-factly mentioned, 'Mrs. Paro Singhal appears to have taken a liking to you.' Reflecting on the gathering, I responded, 'It didn't feel like a party where spouses were being snatched; the crowd exuded friendliness, and they made it quite evident.'

I stopped the car between two street lights and kissed her beautiful lips and said, 'I love you a lot and no woman can ever take your place in my life.' She rested her head on my shoulder as I drove towards her residence.

Chapter Six

I did not meet Amita until the end of June. During the interim days, I decided to open the shutters of the three service centres that my grandpa owned. One at Santa Cruz near to Milan railway underpass which boasted of nearly 25 auto part shops. Grandpa had one of the largest shop cum service centres with 7 mechanics employed. The second shop was near Khar station and the third close to Bandra Station.

All the three centres were well laden and were a sore eye to grandpa's competitors, in fact if any of the nearby shops did not have a particular spare part, they would buy the same from my grandpa and sell it at a profit of 5%. My grandpa never grumbled so long he profited 25%.

I phoned some of grandpa's trusted salesmen and mechanics and asked them to prepare an inventory of all items in the shops along with the MRP written on them.

It took 10 days to finally conclude the exercise and to download onto the tally sheet for each shop.

The guys at the three shops never took me seriously, I never could express myself in Hindi, I could feel it that whatever instructions I gave sounded more like request, they had stamped an impression even when grandpa was alive that I was good for nothing bum, a spoiled rich dude incapable to face a fast moving, street smart, treacherous and conniving, *care a fu*k* attitude youth of my age.

Such guys were wrong just because I didn't follow their style of existence, I could never be rude or think high and mighty of myself. In short, I hate arguing.

The next day I invited my workmen to my house, a total of around 20 of them.

I conducted the meeting in my backyard garden and after serving tea and a few snacks, I called the meeting, 'Those who wish to leave the Company may please stand up. Four stood up and I politely told them that their dues will be settled by mid week and that they were now free to leave my premises.'

The remaining lot looked at me with expectations and I put forward my intentions to run the business efficiently.

Within 20 days, all three centres were running well and independently and overseen by carefully selecting three shops incharge. Being an accounts man I set up a fool proof system for my managers to honestly run my shops, though I would visit the shops twice a day.

At least Amita would not admonish me for doing nothing other than scratching my bums.

'Hi Mahavir how are you?' Amita buzzed me one fine day.

'Well, I am doing good. It's just that the silence has been quite unbearable. It just dawned on me that we haven't had a conversation in the last 20 days. Were you away, perhaps out of town? That's the only explanation I can think of for not receiving a call from you.' Reflecting on my choice of words, I couldn't help but curse myself for offering such an easy alibi. Sometimes, I do act like a real jerk.

'Hey, I am really sorry. Yes, I was out of town. My elder Bhuaji was very ill, thank God she is okay now,' she fibbed, and that shut the subject right on my face.

'I am sorry to hear that. I am glad she is okay now and you are back in town!' I sighed.

'Thanks! Today is Saturday, so… where are you taking me out for dinner?' She asked with much anticipation.

'There is a new restaurant opened at Churchgate called Venice Delight. They make one of the finest thin crust pepperoni and bacon pizzas with a hint of mashed potatoes.'

'I just can't understand how you like that meat? In any case you may have that and I'll help myself with some chicken!' she conceded.

'Sounds good!' I hung up and started getting ready.

I picked Amita outside Regal Cinema and in fifteen minutes we were outside the restaurant and surrendered the car keys at a valet kiosk. I always wondered where my car would be parked on such a busy street? Maybe they tie up with the security of the residential buildings on a rental basis. Who cares as long as I get my car back in one piece.

The waiter approached our table holding an imported French wine bottle wrapped in pure white serviette and then he ceremoniously tilted the bottle and let the blood red pinot gurgle into Amita's Crystal glass and then mine..

'Cheers to this wonderful moment! I have some good news for you.' Amita gave me a sexy smile.

'Are you pregnant?' I just said for fun's sake.

'Idiot I'm not yet married to you neither have we made love!' Please don't try to be an innocent guy.' She said haughtily.

'So tell me the good news.' I pretended to be very curious.

'Dad will be home next week and he wants to meet you.' She waited for my reaction and I surrendered.

'Oh really, what fantastic news! Umm…just a thought, suppose he doesn't like me then how do you plan to handle the situation?' I made a pitiful face and Immediately rewarded with her answer.

'If I tell my father that I like you then he will not oppose and give his consent wholeheartedly.'

I gulped down my wine and while filling my glass, the pizzas arrived with the pepperoni and bacon sizzling over a perfect thin crust. Similarly her chicken tandoori with cheese and potato was also laid.

The pizzas were so tempting that both got engrossed in eating and stopping to take a gulp of the wine before attacking the next triangle. I finished first and she resigned from eating the last triangle which I willingly obliged and in a jiffy had it stuffed down my throat.

I paid the bill and we waited for the car to arrive. The cool Arabian Sea breeze hit on me and I felt light on my feet though not tipsy. I drove the car leisurely and the radio was playing classic love songs and Amita came over and snuggled against me.

I drove fast and parked the car in the parking lot of Chowpatty beach and passionately kissed Amita. I tried to put my hand on her left breast and she slapped my wrist.

I did more kissing and she allowed my hand to explore her cheeks and her neck.

Suddenly, there was a knock on my window and fearing the cops, I looked at the window and saw an urchin knocking on the glass and putting his fingers to his mouth begging for money.

I knew the urchin boy had me by my balls and wouldn't budge so I pulled out my wallet and gave him a tenner which he refused and in desperation he syphoned out a hundred and then left.

I got started on Amita all over again and this time the knock was from the urchin's sister and that brought an end to our kissing session.

I ignited the car and grudgingly dropped Amita at her residence and headed home.

By now, I was on fire but soon realised that Kantabai had quit the job. In a depressing mood, I reached home and soon went to bed with a last thought that I must find a replacement to warm my bed unless …..Amita marries me at the earliest.

The day arrived and Amita buzzed 'Mahavir, dad arrived yesterday and wants to meet you tonight at 7 PM, please do not be late, you know Army men believe in punctuality.' It sounded more like if I'm late the marriage may not take place. Jesus Christ, it's working the opposite way around, isn't the girl side who woos the boy.

Anyway, Amita was well aware that I was a soft target.

At precisely 6:59:30 PM, I rang the bell, and without delay, a robust, well-dressed man with a thick, bushy moustache swung open the sturdy wooden door. 'Mahavir?' he inquired, raising his eyebrows in a silent physical questionnaire. 'Yes, sir,' I replied with my most welcoming smile.

'Come on in, young man and great to meet you. Amita talks about everything good about you. So what would you like to drink, choose your poison?' The Brigadier pointed toward an array of foreign liquor, I suppose, courtesy- Army canteen.

I helped myself to a 30 ML Black label filled with three quarters of water. I was quite aware that the Brigadier's eyes were scrutinising my glass and myself. He poured 60ml for himself and ceremoniously said 'Cheers!' and so we both sipped with the Brigadier making a funny expression on his face which is quite common to persons having the first sip of a large peg.

Soon a middle aged woman, replica of Amita entered the room escorted by two orderlies carrying tandoori *boti* kebabs and another with mutton *sheesh* kebab. I stood up and said, 'Namaste aunty Ji!' She smiled and said, 'Namaste beta!' Amita also joined us and sat next to her mother.

'We have a son named Raghav who is also in the army,' Brigadier Bhatnagar said proudly.

'Tell us about yourself, young man, what do you do?' Six eyes watching me intently.

'I did my post graduation in Accountancy and Finance and was working in a Reality Firm and had to leave the job to tend to my aged grandparents. I was very fond of them. You see sir, my life has been a complicated one so far,' Brigadier stopped me from talking further, he downed his glass and poured a fresh 60 ml plus 10 or 15 ml over it, I could sense things were not going well about me, he didn't offer me to bottom up my glass to pour a fresh one. Once he was ready I continued and spoke about me being an unwanted sibling, about my sisters marrying away, my brothers marrying and settling in different parts of the country, my parents migrating to Chennai leaving me alone to tend and look after my grandparents for whom I became the joy of their life. We three lived happily until first my grandma passed away and within another year my grandpa left me for her heavenly abode. I stopped talking and looked for their reaction.

I heard my supposed future in-laws let out a sigh of disappointment and looked accusingly at their daughter for a spoiled evening by calling home a suitor with no future.

'Mahavir why don't you tell them everything? About your bungalow, your inheritance and the three service stations that you operate?' Amita literally and hysterically appealed to me.

'I didn't find it necessary since you are to marry me and not my bungalow and other inheritance.' I waved my hand in dismissal.

'It is necessary, all parents like their daughters to get married in secured homes with a well to do environment.' She insisted.

I gracefully accepted her appeal and mentioned the inheritance of the bungalow at Juhu and everything that I bequeathed while my grandpa was alive. I saw the ears of the Brigadier prick up like a thoroughbred German Shepherd and his eyes having a happy crinkled glee.

'Let me pour you a drink!'

'It's okay sir, I'll help myself.' I went to the bar and poured a 60ml slug, not caring what they thought. The mood had suddenly become lively with a lot of pampering thrown in.

The party lasted well into the night, I phoned my chauffeur who brought the shining C- Class Mercedes to their doorstep and I waved them goodbye.

I soon imagined the Brigadier shutting the door and doing the action of swinging a fishing rod and winding the pulley to pull up a big catch to which his dear wife gave him a sexy smile.

Chapter Seven

On returning home for lunch after my daily round of visiting the centres, I looked forward to some great lunch the replacement maid prepared,

As I was pouring steaming hot pomfret curry over a mound of brown boiled rice, my phone buzzed. Irritated at the timing, I picked up my mobile and barked,' hello!'

'Hi Mahavir, I'm Mukesh, we met at the party. I'm Paro's husband.' I remembered.

'Hi Mukesh, how are things with you?' I politely replied, though a bit confused.

'Listen, you don't mind if we come over to your house for a drink. We both liked you and it would be fun to get friendly so that once you've married Amita it will be great to hang around together.'

'It's my pleasure and so at what time will you and Paro be coming so that I can tell Amita to join us.'

'Oh we are just coming for half an hour, week days are hectic for me and I avoid late nights. I'll phone Paro to take a cab and reach your house at 7 PM and by that time I should also be there so that later Paro and I can return home together. Is it okay with you, hope we are not piling on you?'

'Don't be silly Mukesh, come over and I look forward to it.' The curry was getting cold.

That same evening after having visited the centre I went to a dry fruit shop and purchased pistachios, salted almonds and roasted cashew nuts along with a packet of Monaco biscuits and Craft cheese spread.

At ten minutes past 7 PM, the front door bell rang and I instantly opened the door to a worried looking Paro who said, 'Hasn't my husband arrived?'

'He should be coming any moment, please come in and feel at ease.' I loved this beautiful lady with such fine features and graceful poise though I sense sadness in her demure. I left the front door open, lest she felt scared of being behind the closed door when her husband arrived. I initiated the talk to avoid an awkward situation.

'So what does Mukesh do, is he in business?'

'Yes he runs a business at Nariman Point, he has a big stationary outlet spread over a full ground floor of a 26 storey building selling stationery essentials along with computer and photocopying and many other office secretarial needs. He is always on his toes in spite of having a staff of 20 employees. He occupies half the ground floor of this huge multi storey building.

'Oh that's a good business and all in cash.' She pulled out her phone and dialled, 'Mukesh where are you? I think I'll go home,'

'Honey I'm on Linking Road and should meet you both in 20 minutes,' I heard Mukesh convinces her and she accepts a Diet Coke, once she hangs up the phone.

'I'm sorry I've put you in an awkward situation, I mean we met just once earlier and here I am with you all alone, hope you don't mind.'

'Not at all, I have good intentions after all I'm marrying your friend Amita so be at ease.' I laughed aloud.

After a few uneasy moments of awkward silence and monosyllabic talk, we heard the car horn, I followed Paro to the main door and gave my broadest smile to Mukesh as he walked in shaking his head in frustration, 'It took me exactly an hour from the Bandra signal, the snail pace on Linking Road and Juhu was frustrating, sorry Paro I kept you waiting.' Mukesh addressed his wife whose face showed the displeasure.

'I think it's late, let's go home.' Paro stood up and I could see her face was determined.'

I realised even if I politely urged her to sit and relax while Mukesh and myself had a drink, it would be torturous and so I took control of the situation,

'Mukesh we'll meet up soon and make up for the time lost.' I stood up and Mukesh followed suit.

I waved them goodbye as the car moved, I was pretty sure that an argument between the two would take place and finally docile Paro would have to shut up.

I quickly got indoors blanketing the hot and humid pre monsoon weather and sat on the sofa wondering what to do. The shops would just about be shutting, it was dark to go for a walk on the beach. I felt tremendously lonely and finally switched on Netflix and watched a movie making sure to avoid drinking as it could turn into a nasty habit. I had a late dinner and soon after the movie I shut my eyes in the folds of my blanket keeping me cosy in the cool air conditioned room.

My thoughts wandered in various directions, I thought about Amita as a person, how she spent the day, which all clients she met and how she would seriously convince a prospective client. I realised that I would never be familiar with her professional aptitude even when married, a complex thought indeed. Our vacations abroad or within the country will be based on her time and convenience.

In my half-asleep state, I found myself pondering over the three shops that were running smoothly and making money on their own. Is this all I'll be doing for the rest of my life? I have plenty of money, a large house, and flashy cars. What else am I searching for? I decided to reflect more on this matter, and with a disheartened mind and droopy eyelids, sleep engulfed me, carrying me into the realm of dreams.

I enjoy the first two hours of the morning. First the 40 minutes of yoga, 30 minutes walking barefoot on Juhu beach and thereafter a 20 minutes swimming. This routine kept me in fit condition even if I lazed around during the day.

The phone buzzed, Amita's melodic voice tuned in, 'Hi Mahavir, what were you doing?'

'I was thinking about you, my love.' I said while piercing a piece of egg, toast and soft bacon and shoving it into my mouth.

'No, you are having your breakfast you liar.'

'I'm having breakfast and was also thinking about you,' I lied. Amita gave up.

'Listen, last evening I got a surprise call from Paro. I hope you remember we met her and husband Mukesh at the party?'

'Yes I remember, so what about it?' I became curious.

'Well she said that four of us will have dinner this Saturday. She wanted us to visit her house but unfortunately Mukesh's father invited his few friends so she suggested that she will outsource mutton Kheema and Bandra pao along with chicken makhani from Minni Punjab and will ask them to deliver at your house by 9:00 pm so that you men can enjoy a few drinks.' Amita waited.

' But why my house? We could go to a restaurant and enjoy some fine dining.'

'It is more fun to sit informally at home and listen to some good ghazals and also know each other more closely and be good friends.' Amita asserted.

'Just 10 days ago, they came home and confused things.' I blurted and then continued telling the whole episode of last time to a confused Amita.

'Why didn't you tell me earlier.' She questioned accusingly.

'I didn't see the need for it.' I retorted.

'You are wrong, knowing everything about another woman is my business, after all we are getting married.' That was like music in my ears and total calm took over.

'I'm sorry but on Saturday please be here at least one hour earlier, I won't be able to handle it.'

'Okay I will,' Amita assured.

On Saturday the four of us settled on the sofas with the drink of our choice and contentment written on our faces. I was especially glad to see Paro enjoying herself and at that very moment I turned to see Amita watching me. I felt that my would-be wife suspected me of having a special interest in Paro.

I went over to the musical console and switched to love duets by lyricist Khayyam on a low decibel just enough audible to set in a romantic environment. Amita stares at me, Mukesh stares at Amita and Paro stares at Mukesh.

'There is a lovely pre monsoon breeze blowing, let's go in the back garden and enjoy the flowers and the garden recently curated as claimed by Mahavir.' Mukesh suddenly got up and others followed suit, though a bit surprised.

Outside was indeed very pleasant with a cool breeze fanning us all and the flower pods swinging in utter joy and carefree indulgence.

'See I told you it will be pleasant!' Mukesh said and the other three agreed in unison.

After finishing our drinks, we headed inside for refills. The atmosphere was light, with jokes flowing freely, and I took the bold step of sharing anecdotes from my initial visit to her home, including a bit of mimicry that elicited laughter from everyone, Amita included. I anticipated her playful rebuke later, but in that moment, the joyous mood prevailed.

'Mahavir you don't mind if I have a smoke in your garden? I'm not regular but at such times I enjoy it.' He started walking towards the back door leading to the garden.

'You could smoke in here, it's okay.'

'I don't like to spoil the environment inside.' Mukesh clarified.

'Yes it's better he smokes outside.' Paro chipped in.

By the time Mukesh came in, the doorbell rang and the food had arrived.

The table was already laid and Amita went and poured the piping hot food in serving bowls. Paro joined her and helped lay the dishes on the table.

In silence all that had been ordered was relished and consumed.

Two portions of caramel custard were consumed by the four of us.

By midnight, Mukesh and Paro wished us an early marriage and left.

Amita quickly cleared the table and put them in the sink for the maid to take care of the next morning.

Finally, she came and settled on the sofa next to me, inviting a serene pause that lingered in the air. The unspoken calm between us created a canvas for shared sentiments, and as we embraced the quietude, it felt like a precursor to the forthcoming exchange of personal stories and heartfelt conversations, ready to unfold in the tranquillity of the moment. I put my left hand round her neck and drew her towards me and kissed her. I loved the breath emanating from her nostrils and her mouth was always honey dew. She allowed me to explore her mouth with my tongue. It's difficult to explain that if her mouth could arouse me tremendously then what would the rest of her body do to me. I dared to put my right hand on her left breast and she allowed me to knead her.

I further tried to explore her stomach area and tried to pry below her navel area and that's when she said in a husky voice to stop. I complied and was happy that I would be getting married to a chaste and an upright woman.

Before long, I chauffeured her back home, and she nestled beside me as we embarked on a comfortable 50-minute drive to her house. The gentle hum of the car enveloped us, creating a cocoon of shared warmth and quiet companionship.

'You have a soft corner for Paro, I saw how you keep looking at her.' Amita broke the silence at one moment. I guess she had too much obsessive thinking getting on to her regarding Paro.

'I think that's the craziest thing that you have said this evening. Being a fellow man I feel mukesh is cheating on his wife and I always find him talking rudely to Paro. I look at her because she seems like a fine lady and does not deserve ill treatment and the beauty is that she does not react emotionally in front of others.'

The discussion concluded with those thoughts lingering in the air, leaving an unspoken understanding between us. As we parted ways, some things remained unspoken, adding a layer of nuance to our evolving connection.

A week later I had the pleasure or shall I say ordeal to be invited for dinner by Brigadier Saab at the Army club. He had a funny habit of stretching his upper lip down and so his toothbrush moustache would also jump up and down and sometimes he would crank his face to right or left with his chin nearly touching his neck. I had the ability to laugh inside me without others realising it.

He welcomed me by demoting me from Maha to just Veer ji. We were sitting nice and cosy with subsidised rate Black Label when suddenly my would-be father in law got up and signalled me by twist of his neck, to join him for a walk on the well manicured lawns. I took my glass and joined him and at the back of me I heard my would be mother in law telling Amita 'you really have got yourself a handsome man' I could not hear how Amita responded because by then I had walked away.

'So young man, I take it that you are serious about marrying my daughter.'

'Sir I mentioned that during our last meeting.'

'I know my son, just trying to assert myself.' I felt like telling that I want to marry his daughter and not him.

'I would like to have a bit of a Zing to your background. For instance when you are asked about your work, running a spare part shop doesn't sound very appealing, I would prefer you saying that you are an industrialist manufacturing Solar energy plant or something like that.' Brigadier concluded.

'Should I establish a plant manufacturing solar panels, even though I have little knowledge about it?' I pondered aloud.

'No, young man! I mean something respectable like owning a hotel, you know what I mean.'

'I'm sorry, but I don't quite grasp your point, although I sense a hint of you trying to stroke your ego. I can't quite align with your line of thinking. Let's return to the table, sir; I need a refill,' the Brigadier expressed, accompanying me back, his upper lip slightly contorted in a downward stretch.

Next day the Brigadier left for Ladakh and during the next full month we had frequent rains. I dined out with Amita, went to many parties and yes we became closer to Mukesh and Paro by regularly meeting.

Chapter Eight

I often find July to be the most unnerving month in Mumbai. Buildings collapse, claiming innocent lives, heavy waterlogging turns roads into a sluggish maze for frustrated car owners, and the constant threat of someone being pulled into an open sewage manhole looms. Diseases and viral infections run rampant. Everyone prays for a respite from continuous rain, haunted by the tragic memory of 800 lives lost during flooding in hutment colonies.

The citizens, weary from navigating the challenges of an office day in semi-wet clothes, returned home to a stifling atmosphere. Nights offered little solace, lacking sufficient sleep to shake off the day's ordeals and be rejuvenated to face the impending challenges the next morning. The unsettling reality sent shivers down my spine.

On the 12th of July, I picked up the newspaper from the pipe container outside the main door and opened the folded paper to read the headline 'LOW PRESSURE CENTRED 75 miles west of Mangalore' may develop into a Tropical storm, presently moving slowly in Northeasterly direction, presently predicted to hit landfall at Mumbai. Anticipated stormy winds reaching speeds of 100 kilometres per hour are approaching. As I immersed myself in reading, the gusts of wind grew stronger, and I could sense their intensifying force. All around, coconut trees swayed vigorously in response to the impending tempest.

Fewer cars than usual were heading southward toward the financial and business sectors of the city, with drivers wary of potential congestion on the return journey. Life in the city of Mumbai had ground to a halt, bringing about a state of standstill.

On the very first day of the storm, I went across to the cold storage across the road and stacked the freezer with a variety of cold cuts like ham, bacon, salami, eggs etc.

None of it required cooking but a cut between two slices and munch away chasing it down with cold coffee or just plain milk.

My nights were a one man entertainment with ghazals, love songs of Amar Prem and extra large pegs of single malt and finally talking to Amita for at least half an hour and later deep sleep with no care of the havoc that was being experienced by my fellow Mumbaikars.

On the fourth night, I got crazy and phoned Amita that I'm driving to her house and pick her up to spend a night at my house, I promised her that I won't rape her and that I just wanted her company.

She became sentimental and I could visualise and sense her emotions and said,

'No darling please don't do that, the whole of Mumbai is suffering so stay home and once it's calm and back to normal, I'll stay a night with you.' She was fibbing but I accepted her reasoning. I turned my car to return and I thought of Babita the failed actress and picked her and brought her home. While it was stormy with gusty winds and Mumbai virtually attacked by the cyclone, I Was drinking, eating, making love and sleeping behind closed doors, continuously for two nights. It was pure bliss and I didn't feel guilty. I presumed it was because of my hormones.

Finally, some respite was apparent when I opened the main door seeing mild drizzle but the thick dark Columbus clouds looked threateningly down on Earth.

The following morning, I was welcomed by brilliant sunshine, even though the Earth hadn't completely absorbed the previous night's rainfall. There remained six inches of water in both the front and backyard garden. Carefully, I tiptoed to the gate, retrieved the newspaper from the makeshift pipe container, and headed inside, closing the door behind me as I eagerly checked the headlines. I was shocked at the disaster. Three buildings in Santa Cruz, Andheri and Jogeshwari had collapsed while the inhabitants slept. Many died being crushed. In many hutment colonies the slumdogs died of electrocution, small infants by drowning, elderly due to cold and hunger. According to the paper, close to 120 humans had perished.

During the day, Amita arrived and took over directing the floor swabbing woman and instructing the washing woman to collect all the soiled clothes and after rinsing them to stuff the clothes in the washing machine. The cook was accordingly given a menu to prepare for lunch and dinner.

Amita spent the full day setting my house in order and finally had two cups of tea prepared and sat next to me and ran her fingers through my hair and saying,

'You poor darling, sorry I could not be by your side these last few days.'

The rains created havoc, the papers are full of destruction. Let alone the city, it was difficult to get out of the house. In fact I had no clue about what was happening in my neighbourhood.'

'Let's talk about pleasant matters, my parents have approved our marriage.

Let's fix the date sometime in December. The weather will be good and outstation guests will be comfortable.'

'Let's go for a walk on the beach, I'm feeling suffocated, I need to be in the open.' The beach was deserted except for a few like minded people like us. The wind was still strong and it looked as if Amita's saree pallu wanted to detach itself and fly away, Amita reined in the pallu and tucked it inside her saree in the stomach region.

It was very romantic as we braved the wind with our hair flying and from time to time we would stop and kiss. I sensed her warmth and desire, and soon we strolled back home together.

I held her and kissed her all over and soon we were undressed and walked towards my bedroom and got into a never ending lovemaking. I thought I was supreme in sex but Amita was a notch above me and consumed me as she wished. Finally it was a shudder, loud cry of satisfaction which finally calmed her. We celebrated three bouts before we saw the dawn peeping through the curtains.

We slept in each other's arms and were awakened by the deliberate clanking of pots. The cook made her presence felt.

54

THE BURIAL

Mukesh and Gayatri - who was a chief accountant in his establishment were in love and had an extra marital relationship. Mukesh was infatuated by her body and started neglecting Paro, his wife. Gayatri kept up her pressure on Mukesh to divorce his wife and marry her.

Mukesh was aware that his parents who were staunch descendants of Jainism and were very fond of Paro and would never allow him to divorce her and any such move would get the wrath of his parents even to the extent of not finally giving the reins of the prosperous business to him and will prefer his younger brother.

As days went by, Mukesh became desperate and one fine day after a lot of deliberation and desperate turmoil, sick in mind and in extreme lust and desire he finally decided to get rid of Paro by getting her killed.

In the last week of June, he gave a lame excuse of stomach infection, skipped his office and instead dressed to see a doctor.

'Why don't you visit Dr. Harshad Shah? I'll dress up quickly and accompany you.' Paro said with concern.

'NO, he rebutted. I'll consult my friend's father who is a known gastroenterologist and just inform dad that I will not be at work today.' Mukesh picked up the car keys and left without looking at his wife.

He drove on till he came to the SV Road junction and then turned left and continued driving until he reached Jogeshwari and took a turn to the left. He kept driving till he reached dadri galli and stopped at a fabrication shop.

A smiling gentleman in vest and lungi greeted him and curiously came near the car, 'Mukesh bhai salaam wale kum!'.

'Malik ko salaam Shaukat.' Mukesh reciprocated. The two of them were classmates in school and later on they maintained their friendship by meeting at least once a month. Presently Shaukat was quite surprised to see his friend. After a few seconds of silence, he asked Mukesh to wait, he went back to his shop and returned dressed in trousers and t-shirt with his head combed and came over to the car and asked him to park a little ahead in a Scrapyard. Asking him to leave his car here so that nobody will scratch the car in vengeance.

They walked over to a small Irani tea stall serving tea and various Iranian tit bits. Shaukat ordered two cups of tea and Naan Khatai biscuits. They indulged in idle talk till the waiter laid their order and left.

'Okay shoot, what's your problem, be honest with me.'

Mukesh shook his head.

'You remember while in the final year you were bullied by two big guys and you finally took the help of a Muslim gangster who beat the shit out of the two boys and never bothered you thereafter. Mukesh reminded Shaukat.

'Yeah I remember, why have you brought that topic today?'

'ell I need his services, a competitor is troubling and threatening us and I need to put him in his place.' Mukesh lied.

'His name is Akhtar Kazi Mohammad, I'll give you his mobile number and you may give my reference and sort things accordingly. Please don't tell me what you want him to do but just keep me out of it.'

The next day, Mukesh dials the number and seeks an appointment with Akhtar Kazi who instructs him to meet him in a restaurant at Andheri junction.

Mukesh was tapped on his shoulder and he lifted his head to see a tall man of 6ft 3inches with a flowing beard minus a moustache staring at him. Sensing his dilemma, the huge mountain of a man said,

'I'm Akhtar bhai and from now on you will not see Shaukat, nor will you try to meet him. He is a fine man and should not be a party to your intentions. Now tell me all.'

Mukesh explains his affair with Gayatri and his intentions to kill Paro.

'When a mind is hell bent to murder his wife, he also works on various options on how he intends to do this act, so have you worked out a strategy? Let me hear your modus and then work out how to go about it.

They walked across the street and came to a single storey house with a broad outdoor veranda. The house was typically painted in green with a clothes line covered with hijabs, kurtas and pyjamas stringed for drying.

'Okay, now start talking.' Akhtar bhai ordered.

Mukesh explains his love affair and expresses a strong desire to end his marriage with desperation.

'Recently I've made friends with a guy who lives at Juhu close to the main beach. He inherited a lot of wealth along with this bungalow built on an 800 sq mtr. plot having a backyard garden. He lives alone and a security guard is stationed day and night who sits in a security room built next to the gate.' Mukesh looks at Akhtar to check if he is following his conversation.

'Go on I'm listening,'

'I want the body to be buried in the garden of this house.' Akhtar looks hard at Mukesh and wonders whether he is talking to a mad person.

'So you want us to take your wife to this bungalow, murder her and then dig a hole and bury her while the security guard and maybe some neighbours are watching us doing the job. Are you crazy by any chance?' By now Akhtar was in anger for having wasted his time. Mukesh hurriedly continued,'Akhtar bhai, I run a large organisation and I'm not a fool, in fact quite intelligent in planning things. You have to listen to the full scheme and then come to a conclusion, am I clear?'

'Till now you have not yet impressed me, but do continue.'

' We are now in monsoon season and every year we get a bout of heavy rains which paralyse Mumbai for a couple of days. Water logging, suburban trains stopped midway, water entering shops etc etc. I am not talking of the kind when 800

Mumbaikars died. I am talking about yearly occurrences. I intend to wait for just such an opportunity when we strike. Hopefully the guard is absent, the heavy rains will keep all windows shut and then a gang of 4 persons will dig a grave of 6ftx4ft and after dumping the body, the men cover up the grave and level the ground by hard press and are driven away in a tempo.' Mukesh ended his plan of action. Akhtar showed some respect to Mukesh but there were many questions still to be asked.

'So I should have at least four men on standby with all digging gear like pickaxes, spades, raincoats etc. what will you pay for this assignment?'

'What do you want, you tell me?' Mukesh asked.

Akhtar thought for a considerable time and said, 'Forty lacs, hope you understand the risk involved. You will pay ₹10 lac advance and balance on completion. Two Jio phones with fictitious names and addresses will be purchased and when you come to pay the advance, one Jio phone will be handed over to you. Tomorrow we will also discuss how to end your wife's life. Akhtar got up signalling the end of the meeting.

'Meet me tomorrow at 10 am outside Dena Bank on the main road at Irla for your advance and to sit somewhere for final discussions.' The two departed.

Mukesh halted at a restaurant and had idli and dosa before going home and didn't have lunch while his wife felt concerned about her sick husband.

The next day Mukesh removed ₹10 lacs from his locker in the Bank and when he came out, Akhtar was standing next to his car. Mukesh asked him to sit in the car next to him and handed him the cash. They drove some distance and entered a restaurant and over a cup of coffee the plan was discussed in minute details and soon after Akhtar left the restaurant and five minutes later Mukesh got into his car and drove towards his office.

It started drizzling and soon intensified into rain. The hot road cooled, disbursing light steam.

Fifteen days later while Mukesh and his father were waiting for lunch which they normally eat at 11am, his father who was reading the newspaper looked at Mukesh and said, 'Looks like we are going to have heavy rains, the paper mentions that a low pressure has formed West of Mangalore and may intensify into a cyclone which is moving in a North Easterly direction.'

Looking up he showed concern and continued, 'I hope we are spared of the type that hit Mumbai and killed more than 800 citizens a few years ago.' The lunch was laid and the two of them got up with a silent sigh and proceeded towards the table.

Later, they took the lift to the parking bay and went towards their individual cars and proceeded to the same business establishment. Mukesh's younger brother Manoj would arrive early and hold the fort. Greeting each other they entered their separate cabins. It was raining outside.

Once Mukesh was settled, he pulled out his mobile and switched to IMD App.

He saw the isobaric circle of the low pressure area, he couldn't understand the yellow and red patches surrounded by lines though he could make out that the centre had moved North in the West region of Karwar. He looked outside his window and noticed that the wind speed had escalated.

It was a dull day of trading and early evening they shut shop and left for home. Manoj lived separately at Bandra with his wife and daughter.

The evening News channels confirmed that the low pressure had intensified into a cyclone and put fear in Mumbai citizens. Heavy rains, thunder and lightning and near darkness could be described as the environment.

The news cautioned that the cyclone centre was moving at a speed of 10 Knots and was expected to hit landfall about 100 Kilometres North of Mumbai in the next 72 hours. Cautionary orange signal was hoisted indicating that the Port of Mumbai was closed for shipping and movement of small crafts, motor launches etc was banned. That night the naked body of his lady love Gayatri lingered in front of his eyes. He turned in the opposite direction from his wife and shut his eyes to try and sleep.

The next morning it was a catastrophe, heavy rains were lashing horizontally with coconut trees swinging violently. The wind was so strong that it was impossible to open any of the windows in their 500 sq metre apartment. To top it all none of the servants had arrived and his wife Paro and his mother were in the kitchen preparing the lunch.

Mukesh switched on the tv but no channels were broadcasting due to signal interruption. He checked his mobile app and learnt that the whole of Mumbai is shut for today and tomorrow and the cyclone would hit landfall day after tomorrow by afternoon. All citizens were warned to stay indoors. He conveyed the news to his family.

That day passed by talking about various relatives and answering worried calls from various cousins and friends from out of State.

In the evening they watched a Hindi movie on HotStar and after dinner the men folks hung around till the kitchen was sorted and by 10 PM they retired to their respective bedrooms.

Mukesh pulled out his briefcase and pretended to be busy with paperwork. The nervousness had set in and a thin layer of sweat covered his face. Paro did not notice since she was busy talking to her mom and sister who lived in Ujjain.

At 5 minutes to 11 PM, Mukesh looked up from his papers and as Paro came out of the bathroom he requested,

'Paro please do me a favour, I've left some important documents in the glove compartment, please can you get them from the car? Babuji wants the three monthly reports tomorrow morning.' Mukesh said without looking up as if too engrossed in his paperwork.

'No I won't go since it's late and I'm not dressed well,' Paro retorted.

'Darling the car is just next to the lift, please wear your nightgown and take the car keys with you. Also open and shut the main door very softly, I'll open the door when I hear the lift pause on our floor. Honey just do this small favour.'

Paro allowed her anger to manifest, donning her night robe as she picked up the keys from the table. She stomped out of the room, opened the main door with care to avoid noise, and gently clicked it shut. Entering the lift, she pressed the button for the parking level, a decision that, in fact, led her towards her unfortunate fate. Poor Paro.

The lift door opened and she didn't realise when strong fingers pressed her mouth and an accomplice wound a rope around her neck and snuffed the life out of the body. The noose kept the pressure till the body finally urinated.

The keys of the car were taken from her hand and bending low between the cars the body was transferred across the wall and laid in the tempo and within minutes the white four wheeler Tempo vehicle moved and took the direction of main Juhu beach.

There was no way anyone would have heard the vehicle start over the noise of the rain lashing accompanied with lightning and thunder.

Time was of essence. Within half an hour, the vehicle stopped at the gate of Mahavir's house. A lookout man who was stationed reported to Akhtar that the security guard was absent.

Ever so stealthily, the main gate was opened and five men carrying digging gear and the body moved to the back garden. They surveyed the area and decided to move the flower pots and dig a grave at that spot. Quickly, a bamboo tent was erected to control the rain water entering the dug area.

Two huge and strong men dug hard, the earth was a soft mixture of mud and sand so digging was faster and the other two used spades to clear the mud. They changed position and relentlessly dug for two hours until a grave of 6x4 ft was ready. The body was gently lowered in the makeshift grave and covered with the mud extracted and a heavy steel planer with a wooden stump was used to compress the earth.

The extra mud left due to the body taking the space, was spread around a substantial area and they were quite sure the rain would even out the mud.

Finally, they replaced the flower pots to their original spots. They collected their gear and silently walked off and assembled in the tempo and drove off.

They drove through Irla flyover and took the highway and every two kilometres they threw the pick axes and the spades and by the time they reached Andheri, Akhtar asked all of them to get off the vehicle and walk away to their homes.

He parked the vehicle at the same place from where he had stolen for a few hours and went home, took a bath and sat down for prayers asking for forgiveness.

At 6:00 am, Mukesh violently knocked on the door of his parents. His mother opened the door and looked at the ashen face of her son who hysterically said,

'Ma is Paro sleeping in your room? I suddenly got up and saw that she was not next to me. I've seen the whole apartment and I can't find her so lastly I disturbed you.

Now that the act of killing was done, Mukesh genuinely regretted his act but it was too late now and his face emitted grief.

Finally Mukesh's dad called the Santa Cruz Police station and within 20 minutes a posse of police headed by sub inspector knocked on their door and recorded their statement.

'We will send a search team including sniffer police dogs and hopefully have some results very soon.' They left the apartment after instructions to a constable to stay on guard and not allow anybody including neighbours, servants or friends to enter the apartment.'

Cursing the heavy rains, very strong winds pushing them from approaching their van, the police team finally sat in their van and left to report the full matter to Dy. Sp.Of Police Ramesh Mhatre.

The cyclone had hit landfall and wind speed of 100Km/ hour lashed the city. All infrastructure could not be accessed due to flooding., reports of trees being uprooted. Collapse of a few old buildings with a few residents buried under the debris, the havoc was experienced all over Mumbai.

The file about a citizen named Paro Singhal missing was presently not on the priority list. There were more serious and deserving disasters that needed immediate attention.

In the meantime, a missing person ad with Paro's photo and a reward was printed in all the newspapers and in the afternoon editions of dailies.

The news took prominence two days after the rain had stopped and Singhal's family refused to take any phone calls except of the very near relatives. It was indeed an extraordinary incident which attracted abundant mystery.

No progress had yet been made by the Police department until Mukesh's father personally met the SHO and worked out an understanding so that the case is taken on priority. As the wheels of justice began to turn, the investigation gained momentum, weaving a complex web of intrigue and suspense that would shape the course of the unfolding narrative. Little did they know that the journey ahead would unravel hidden truths and cast a revealing light on the intricate threads of human relationships.

Aftermath of the burial

Chapter Nine

Two days after the rains had stopped I watched from my side window, the sun glimpsed from in between clouds racing by, I noticed the gardener open the gate and go towards the backyard garden.

Some time later, the gardener pressed the bell at the front door. I answered, stepping outside and stretching my arms with a hearty yawn.

'Saab I'll come after two days, there is still 4 inches of water and hopefully it should dry by the day after tomorrow.'

'Okay, as you say Mali ji,' I shut the door and went inside.

Once inside, my phone buzzed and Amita was on line, 'Honey, have you read the news?'

'No, I haven't glanced at a newspaper in the past four days, and I have no inclination to delve into them, brimming with news of diverse disasters ,anyway, why do you ask me? What did you read?' I said.

'Well have you heard that Paro left her house a few nights ago and that she is missing or rather untraceable, Jesus what could have happened?'

'What are you saying? I hope your rumour mongering friends may have cooked up the story.' I interjected.

'There was a missing person ad posted by Mukesh Singhal with Paro's photo printed in all the newspapers with a reward mentioned. I'm sending you a screenshot of the ad.'

I remained silent and perplexed at this unexpected news. Upon picking up my mobile, a buzz was sent to Mukesh, but it went unanswered, receiving no response.

I went to my bedroom and shook Babita, the failed actor with whom I romped for a couple of nights squeezing me dry! And now… looking at her in blissful satisfaction suffocated me! I opened all the windows to get rid of our body odour and said, 'Hey Babita! I suggest you dress up now and leave, my girlfriend phoned and I think she is on her way over here.' Babita was all sport and quickly freshened and while going I shoved a few thousand currency notes in her hand and she retorted,

'I'm not a fucking whore, you bastard!'

'Honey don't think in that direction, I like you and would love that you buy a branded fancy dress for yourself.' She seemed convinced at my overture, took the money and left.

Soon the cleaning bai came and I instructed her to clean up my room first and later tackle other rooms. She gave me a puzzled look but did as told.

The doorbell once again chimed and it was a pleasure to see Amita stomping in and falling straight in my arms. We kissed and then she gave me an appreciative smile and said,

'You just had a shower? You smell nice!' She flopped on the sofa and suddenly an unintended air of worry surrounded her aura. She signed and then said, 'I wonder where Paro is, how can she just disappear ditching her husband?'

'Honey please don't speak ill about her, without knowing the facts.' I retorted but kept quiet after realising immediately that it was going to be used against me.

Well, she did! You know girls are quick to do that! They are made that way! It made me smile though!

'I know you had a soft corner for her.' I let it pass and kept quiet.

We had lunch together and she left for an appointment with a client and I decided to visit my three showrooms having fitment space for two cars at the back. Exclusive and expensive cars need good workmen to install the parts.

No business was transacted during the week. Things will improve only after Monday, tomorrow being a Sunday and my thoughts went towards Amita who had promised to spend the Sunday with me.

The next day, as promised, Amita spent the day with me. I bought some mutton from a nearby butcher and she prepared it the Punjabi style; reminding me of my grandma, who prepared mutton on every Sunday, as a ritual. Amita made small lachha parathas and then crisped them in the Oven to give a tandoori touch.

After lunch, we lay down on bed and she allowed heavy petting but refused the ultimate wish by saying, 'We did it once and the next one will be on the night we get married and thereafter whenever you wish.'

The mystery of Paro's disappearance was the next topic that we discussed, 'They must have had a massive fight and let me tell you that Mukesh always mistreated her, the poor girl was always very subdued and relenting to his tantrums,' I declared, heatedly.

'I said earlier, you always had a soft corner for her, she had this pretty sad looking beautiful face which could melt the heart of the toughest Chaste men.' She opined.

'Women, jealousy is thy name!' I laughed.

The next topic we discussed was our marriage, which venue to choose and who all to be invited. I clearly made it known to her not to expect any of my relatives including my immediate family i.e. my parents and my brothers and sisters and so it will be a one sided show with all her relatives and me alone.

I suggested, 'We could have a private marriage havan - performed by an Aryasamaj pandit and then have a reception in a five star hotel.'

'Let me think and discuss with my mother.' She retorted.

Fresh and rejuvenated, I woke up on Monday following a full day spent with my future wife. I told the maid to open all the doors and windows to allow fresh air to enter the house. I saw the gardener level the ground which was uneven at many places around the flower pots that may have been displaced due to heavy rain.

I whistled to my neighbour, Mr Ranjit Malhotra's two lovely Labrador dogs, one brown one, named Ranger and one off white, called Regal.

The Mali worked on alternate days in our two gardens and had heaped up mud in a corner in both houses to facilitate the dogs to cross over, sometimes the Gardner would also cross over from that corner.

The dogs came running at me playfully and I moved my hands over their fur. The poor fellows must have been kept inside in some sheltered balcony during the past few days of havoc.

Satisfied, they sprinted towards the gardener, seeking more love and attention. But very soon the dogs got distracted and started smelling the ground along the pots, they started scratching the ground as if trying to dig. The gardener shooed them away who jumped over the wall back to their bungalow.

'Maybe they smelt a rat or a snake hole.' The gardener looked at me and clarified.

The next morning, my doorbell chimed while I was having my breakfast. It was the gardener and before I could say that today was his day off to work at the neighbours, he yelled.

'The dogs have dug a foot deep hole around the flower pots saab, please complain to Malhotra saab to rein in his dogs.'

I phoned my neighbour, 'Malhotra saab, your dogs are ruining my garden, please do something about it.'

'Mahavir ji, I'll just come and see, I'm quite surprised at their behaviour?'

Malhotra came through the main gate and saw the hole dug by his dogs. He apologised and assured me that he would do something about it and that if they did it again then both will have to remove the heap of mud on opposite corners which will make it impossible for the dogs to cross over.

Malhotra was kind enough to instruct the gardener to firstly fill up the hole before starting to work in his garden.

The following day, there was a recurrence, but with greater damage as they overturned a couple of flower pots. Additionally, the two dogs dug up a hole nearly two feet deep and roughly three feet wide.

Now it had become a matter of concern but being good neighbours we agreed to remove the mud from our respective corner. The mud was again levelled and the possibility of recurrence was snubbed.

CHAPTER Ten

Before lunchtime, I visited each of my showrooms, and afterward, I headed home.

Upon parking my car inside the gate, I noticed two policemen waiting. Meanwhile, my front door opened, and my cook, who went berserk looking at something, started blubbering.

'Saab they are here for two hours, I told them to come after 1PM, they refused.'

'Since the food is cooked, you can go home,' I said to my cook in Marathi.

I invited the two policemen into my living hall and made them sit.

'Yes constable saab how can I be of assistance?' I looked at the senior of the two.

'There has been a complaint that the neighbour's two dogs have been persistently digging in a certain area of your garden.'

'Constable saab, I've not made any complaints. The matter has been resolved and the neighbour has been kind enough to rectify the same.' I clarified.

'Yes sir, we know that and your gardener has explained to us but on receiving a complaint we need to investigate the matter and we hope you have no objection to bringing our police dogs to sniff around. It may turn out to be a hole made by a large rat or a snake or even a mongoose, normally they make holes during monsoon but a complaint needs to be attended to.'

'Yes you may call for your dog squad, I have no objections.' I looked through my window and saw my neighbour standing at his upper balcony and watching.

The senior constable pulled out his mobile and seemed to be speaking to his boss and on getting instructions he shut the mobile and said to me, 'The station is sending two sniffer dogs and will be here in an hour or two so can we sit here or should we wait outside.' I showed courtesy and made them sit while I went to the dining table out of view of the constables and ate my lunch.

Two German shepherd dogs arrived with their leash being held by strong police handlers and soon all of us headed towards the garden. The handlers just kept on following the dogs as they commenced smelling the ground. The moment they neared the flower pots, the dogs pulled on their leash and suddenly sniffed and pawed at the mud.

The sub inspector gave instructions to two constables and the gardener to move the flower pots away and once the area was cleared, the dogs became excited and began digging the soft mud.

The inspector phoned his boss at the police station and explained the situation.

'The Inspector saab is sending four labourers to dig up the affected spot.' The sub inspector informed me and now I sort of got curious about all that was happening.

Within 45 minutes, the labourers started digging. Pick axes were not required as the mixture of sand and mud was loose and the spade sufficiently did the job.

After digging the area 2ft, the dogs were brought and this time they barked and pawed the earth. The labourers dug another foot and the dogs persisted so they dug further and very soon everyone noticed the pink cloth.

The sub inspector cautioned the labourers to dig gently and very soon the body of a woman was unveiled.

'Oh God it's Paro.' I shouted in disbelief.

'I've done nothing, I have done nothing.' I started crying hysterically looking at the crowd around, who all stared at me accusingly.

The sub inspector phoned the police station and within 15 minutes I heard the siren of a police car and I urinated in my trousers. A two star inspector assessed the body in the makeshift grave and phoned the SHO, his boss and appraised him of all that he inspected.

'The coroner is on the way and after he has inspected and made his report, I'm afraid I will be hauling you to the police station. In the meantime, I suggest you lock up your house to prepare for a long absence and yes you can phone anybody and inform them about your situation.'

'Can I call for my advocate to come over?'

'Sure it's your right.' The inspector agreed.

I dialled Mr. Seth and briefly appraised him of my situation. He interrupted me, 'Mahavir I'm not a criminal lawyer however I'll get in touch with Miss Vandana Malik to go over to your place and represent you accordingly, I only hope she is traceable and free to attend your matter.'

I switched off and pocketed my mobile.

A huge crowd had collected outside my bungalow. Things were moving fast, the TV channel vans had appeared from nowhere, press reporters were pushing one another to be in the forefront.

'Hey Bhagwan, how did all of this happen?' I started crying hysterically and the unfortunate part was that I had no one by my side to understand my dilemma.

The coroner arrived along with a police photographer. Upon his instructions, the body was lifted out of the alleged grave and after various inspection, he gave instructions to get the body transferred to the morgue to ascertain the cause and time of death by carrying out the postmortem. The body was slipped into a body bag and the four labourers carried it to the waiting ambulance which left the site immediately.

I went through the whole house and bolted all the doors and windows. I packed two sets of clothes along with essentials such as toothpaste, brush, a cake of soap etc. I bolted all the rooms on the ground floor and as I came out of my bedroom with the personal effects slung in an air bag, a distinguished looking lady in a white saree approached me and handing me a printed form and said,

'I'mVandana Malik & Mr. Seth has requested me to represent you. Please sign this *Vakalatnama* so that I may advise you accordingly.'

I signed the same,

'I didn't do anything, I'm not a murderer.' I cried and pleaded desperately.

'Say nothing now, they will take you to Juhu Vile Parle police station, I will be following you in my car and will be present while the police prepare the *Panchnama* and formally arrest you and then you may explain all the circumstances that led to your present situation.' She said as a matter of factly.

The police jeep stopped at a fairly large independent structure and in front was painted JVPD Police station. A policeman opened the door and ordered me out of the jeep and holding my wrist led me towards the entrance of the station. I felt the sudden urge to disengage my hand from the policeman and run away but better sense prevailed and I trudged along.

As I entered I witnessed a melee of crooks, some sitting opposite senior constables recording statements and preparing the FIR, others were sitting and waiting for their turn. There were also two separate constables recording complaints.

I felt pity for all the policemen carrying out this frustrating work but soon reversed my opinion because I had heard that here is where the origin of money making starts during a criminal's journey to a matter going to court, argued as prepared by the inmates of the station in order for the prosecutor to argue the case and finally based on reports, cross examination and final arguments, the judge announces whether the accused is guilty, including the tenure of jail sentence which may be lenient or harsh depending on the money dished out. Many times even an innocent person has to shell out money so that his or her case is truthfully prepared by the police department.

My matter was high profile and so I was whisked into an inspector's cabin where a mean looking officer welcomed me by first scrutinising me from head to toe and gauging how much loot can be extracted from me.

As I sat, there was a knock on the door and my advocate entered the room and introduced herself and thereafter sat in a chair by my side. I let out a sigh of relief.

The atmosphere was tense and I could see that the inspector was irritated on seeing Vandana Malik but kept his cool and with a broad smile said,

'Advocate Vandana ji, glad to see you, somehow you present yourself in so many high profile cases, welcome madam.'

'Thank you inspector Ashok Gawas.' Advocate Vandana said pleasantly, 'you may please start preparing your report.' The inspector nodded, cleared his throat and said,

'Do you recognise the victim?'

'She is Mrs. Paro, wife of Mukesh Singhal.'

'Did you know her and her husband?'

'Yes they were friends and that's how I recognise the victim.'

'For how long have you known them?' Inspector Gawas leaned forward

'About a month and a half, though we all met and spent the evening about four times.'

'Answer what is asked, don't volunteer information!' my advocate cautioned me.

'Did you fall in love with Paro Singhal or shall I ask were you two in romance?'

'What an absurd question, I am in love with Amita and we are working on a date for marriage, Inspector saab.'

'Mahavir, just answer the question! Were you having an affair with Paro, rather were you in love with her, stick to the point?' Advocate Vandana cautioned him again.

'No, I was not in love with Mrs. Singhal.' I clarified and the inspector gave a wry smile.

'Did you kill the victim?'

'No, I did not.'

'But the body was found in your backyard!' the inspector stressed.

"So, if a dog defecates on your front door, is it automatically assumed that you did it?" I responded, accusingly.

'Mister don't be a smart Alec with me, I will keep you in lock-up for a long time, do you understand?'

'Mahavir, you are at a police station, don't be rude. The inspector is doing his job and is entitled to ask any question that he may feel relevant.' Advocate Vandana whispered or rather hissed in my ear.

'I'm sorry sir.' The inspector was satisfied.

'Where were you on the 16th night?'

'I was sleeping in my house, it was stormy outside and practically the whole of Mumbai was indoors.'

In the next four hours, I was literally asked a thousand questions and the inspector prepared the *Panchnama* over 50 full scape lined pages. I signed the document as suggested by my advocate. A photocopy of the same was handed to me which I passed on to Ms. Vandana.

'Mr. Mahavir Batra, the police are charging you with the murder of Mrs. Paro Singhal. You will be produced before a Judge in a criminal court and seek your remand while we investigate and collect evidence. Until then you will be under lockup in this police station.'

'Constable Nadkarni, come and take this prisoner and put him in the lock-up room.' The constable must have been standing just outside the room for he was quick to enter and signalled me with his head to follow him. I started crying and hollered loudly that I'm innocent.

'Inspector saab, my client is of a high social standing, he has never faced such a situation which may affect him mentally so I request you to please make him sit in the corridor and later sleep out the night and escort him to court tomorrow.' Adv. Vandana requested .

'I request please don't lock me up.' I gently pleaded and made a sign that I would pay up later on. Inspector Gawas gave instructions to the constable accordingly.

The evening progressed into the night which was truly a nightmare. Drunks were hauled in and beaten up to sober them and then pushed into one of the cells which was already brimming with pickpockets, petty thieves, and of course the local *gundas*. It was a pathetic sight and a tough job for the police team on duty.

Later, the kind policeman allowed me to order a pizza for my dinner. I placed an order for the two of us. Later sometime during the night, the same policeman nudged me and offered me to lie on one of the empty benches.

Early morning, I was rudely shaken up by Inspector Gawas,

'Get up! This is not your bungalow, freshen up and be ready to be taken to court to register the FIR and start legal proceedings against you.' I again started crying.

'Now stop those crocodile tears, you should have thought ten times before committing the gruesome murder of an innocent lady.'

'I didn't murder her, I will keep saying so till my last breath,' I shouted at the inspector. Everybody in the outer hall was watching my outburst and they also watched as Gawas gave me a tight slap in order to bring me back to my senses.

Having freshened up and having put on a clean white shirt, I was led into a waiting police jeep with a constable sitting on either side of me and inspector Gawas sitting next to the driver.

I was led to the 1st floor of the Session Court in Goregaon, the whole corridor was infested with lawyers, clients, under trials, murderers, rapists, robbers and innocent citizens. Courtroom 3 was packed with humans as in a suburban compartment during early morning rush hours.

Inspector Gawas shouted for people to move to make way for me to be led towards the area reserved for the accused.

Raising my gaze, I surveyed the room, feeling the weight of accusing eyes fixed upon me. The collective glares already deemed me guilty, casting their judgement even before the Judge assumed his seat. A palpable tension hung in the air, painting a daunting atmosphere that I would have to navigate carefully.. Mobiles and cameras clicked incessantly, capturing the scene even before the Judge had arrived to put an end to the charades. The courtroom buzzed with activity, as if the lens itself held the power to freeze time and document the unfolding drama. I refused to cover my face to avoid identification, who cares what people thought, I knew I was innocent. I looked around and saw my advocate already sitting and she waved at me which gave me some solace.

The door for the Judge opened and then it was pin drop silence as if the screening of the latest blockbuster were to start, I could feel myself drowning in the judgemental glances, when suddenly I heard the bailiff shout with authority 'll rise!' and once the Judge had acknowledged and instructed all to be seated, the bailiff announced 'ow hearing case no. 5546 State of Maharashtra versus Mahavir Batra!'

'State your case.' The judge instructed the prosecutor to proceed explaining the matter. The prosecutor was a tall man with a thick bushy moustache, a mean looking overconfident individual who gave the impression of never having lost a case. I thought and whispered to myself 'Well Mr. Prosecutor, this is one case I will not let you win.'

'My lord! A gruesome murder has been committed by the accused, Mr. Mahavir Batra who ruthlessly murdered the victim Mrs. Paro Singhal and had the audacious guts to bury her in his backyard garden.' The prosecutor meticulously recounted the entire incident, culminating in the revelation of the body unearthed from a grave measuring 6 feet in length, 4 feet in width, and 5 feet in depth.

'I therefore, request your lordship to charge him under section 300 and 302 and deny bail to the accused and hold in custody until all evidence is collected and the alleged murderer is formally charged and the case presented.' Confidently, the prosecutor turned his gaze towards the judge and then swept his eyes across the crowd in the hall, wearing a triumphant demeanour as if he had just conquered a country. In search of praise and admiration, he scanned the room, basking in the perceived success of his argument.

My advocate Vandana Malik stood up. She had her thick hair combed back into a high ponytail tied with an ornamental hair clip. She wore dark eyeliner that emphasised her large prominent eyes and her lips needed just a touch of lipstick to give a contrast to her very fair face. She stood up straight and the short black official jacket could barely camouflage her well endowed breasts and even her hourglass figure was a treat for the spectators in the full court hall. I felt as if she purposefully stood in silence as if thinking but in fact allowing all, including the judge to appraise her persona. It seemed her way to pull the crowd to her side.

'How do you plead, Mr. Batra?' The judge looked at me for an answer.

'Judge saab, I've never thrown a stone at a stray dog let alone killing a human, sir I'm being framed!' I shouted while letting the tears run down my cheeks.'

'Order, order! I don't want any theatrics in my court. Tell your client to behave or else I will file a contempt of court.' The judge looked at my advocate, threateningly.

'Sir, my client declares not guilty.' Adv. Vandana answered on my behalf.

'This murderer is guilty and he should be hanged.'

'Who said that? stand up!' the judge looked around and saw a youth standing up.

'My lord I am Mukesh Singhal, the aggrieved husband of the deceased, this man deserves no mercy, after your death sentence to him, he will go to hell.'

'Young man, do not disturb the court proceedings. Another outburst and I will debar you from the courtroom, whatever you wish to say, let your advocate speak!'

'The court gives the accused seven days of judicial custody to prepare their evidence and be ready for trial, case adjourned!'

'If I may request your honour for a 15 days custody, the case needs intensive investigation to collect evidence.' The prosecutor requested.

'Motion denied, the court will meet again on Monday. Next case please.'

Nobody was interested in the next case and with a final accusing glance at me and a hungry look at Vandana, the crowd and press reporters dispersed.

While being led out of the courtroom Advocate Vandana came over to me and consoled me and assured me that she would come over to the police station the next day and discuss certain matters and in the meantime not to talk or answer questions to the police without her presence.

On the way to the police station, I asked Inspector Gawas if I could draw some money at an ATM.

'Why do you need the money?'

'To give here and there and some for ordering some food.' I said directly looking at the inspector who remained silent and finally making a decision, he instructed the driver to stop at an ATM kiosk.

I withdrew ₹25,000 and stashed it in both my pockets. Upon reaching the station, I requested Inspector Saab to meet him in his office. Once inside alone, I discreetly handed over ₹20,000 to him.

'So this is all? You asshole you think we come so cheap, I have my seniors and they have their seniors to look after.' Gawas glared at me.

'Saab you tell me what you want and that figure I can only give once I'm on bail.'

Inspector realised that I could withdraw a limited amount from the ATM.

'Okay fine, we will wait until then and the figure is twenty lacs and that doesn't end here. You will appreciate that a lot of reports have to be made on which your case will be based.'

I kept quiet though well aware that I will have to shell out a lot of money.

The next day Advocate Vandana breezed in bringing hope, I had no one else I could Bank on.

'Vandana Ji, May I use your phone?'

'Whom do you want to call?'

'My girlfriend,' Vandana gave her phone and I dialled the number I knew by heart.

'Hello, Amita speaking.' I could sense the trauma in her voice.

'Amita this is Maha……..' the phone was disconnected and I looked at my advocate and then at the phone.

'What did you expect that she would say hello darling how are you doing after murdering Paro, oh I miss you? Well let me tell you that you are hot news on all newspaper dailies. No girl would want to have anything to do with you, I would stay away from a man I trusted who is charged with murder.' She admonished me.

'I have met inspector Gawas and have requested him to go easy on you, he has his limitations, you are lucky that you are in Judicial custody and not in a proper jail. Now you tell me all that transpired during those three days of stormy conditions which lashed the city with heavy, squally rains.'

I told advocate Vandana everything, that I stayed indoors for three days and then about the dogs and I questioned Vandana as to why I would call out for the dogs after rains if I had dug up a grave and a body lay in it.

'Have you any proof that you did not leave your house during those three nights in particular?' This is one question I dreaded the most. I'll have to drag in the name of Babita, my part time lover. What would Amita think and what impression will the lacs of newsreaders have about me and not forgetting the presiding judge whose impression would be the most vital. I felt I was doomed.

'Yes I have an alibi, I had a friend who stayed at my place during those three nights.' My advocate adjusted her posture with alertness written on her face.

'Go on, tell me all.' She insisted.

'I have a part time girlfriend, with the gloomy weather approaching I stopped by her residence and invited her to spend a few days at my house. She agreed.'

'So the three days of cyclonic conditions, murder and burial, the two of you were romping in bed, making raunchy love, not knowing what was happening in your backyard?' She thrashed at me.

'Everyone in Mumbai, especially along the beaches, is aware that it is extremely difficult to open your doors, Mumbai is paralysed.' I ended shamelessly.

She soon got up and said that she will meet in court on Monday during my bail hearing, and I could sense that her gait had a confused walk, probably surmising my character.

The four days at the police station had taken a toll on my mental health. I looked dishevelled and convincingly looking like a criminal as I brushed my teeth and looked at myself in the cracked mirror of the washroom.

On Monday, the courtroom was packed, a couple of policemen had to literally use force to make way for us. I did get a few slaps on my head by the general public venting out their hate for me. Finally I was seated on the bench reserved for the accused.

While waiting, I anxiously wondered if the day would pan out favourably. I shuddered thinking the opposite.

Soon the judge arrived and after the customary rituals, the bailiff read out the case number and the judge asked the prosecution lawyer to proceed.

The prosecutor started off with the re run of the same narration from the last hearing and further attempted to base his arguments on the fact that the body of the victim was found on my premises and that I knew the victim when alive and that I should be charged forthwith and put in jail during the proceedings of the case. My lawyer was quick on her feet and gave a distressed look at the judge and said, 'My lord! Under the law my client is presumed innocent until proven guilty. The honourable court has primarily laid utmost importance on evidence and ironically concrete evidence against my client has been the missing ingredient in the tall claim made by the learned prosecution today.' Adv. Vandana fumed audibly while looking at the judge and a general glance at the spectators in the courtroom and then continued, 'Nothing of what the prosecution has stated today, raises even the slightest of reasonable doubt on my client's involvement in the matter.' Advocate Vandana said, her palms resting flat on the table, fixed her gaze directly on the judge, awaiting his reaction.

'Respond to the defence lawyer's claim.' The judge looked at the prosecutor to argue.

'My lord! We need more time to gather evidence. The accused is clever and we need to unravel his misdeeds.' At this juncture, my advocate interrupted and reiterated her earlier remark and said,'We are all here in the interest of the delivery of justice for which conclusive evidence is a matter of great importance and justice cannot be rushed. However, considering my client's lack of any prior criminal record, upstanding status in the society and high moral character which drives him to aid this honourable court to deliver justice.Arguing against the necessity of keeping my client in custody, it appears frivolous, considering he poses no flight risk. Residing in a bungalow, managing his own business, and overseeing substantial properties throughout the city, my client is well-established. Furthermore, attending hearings as required would pose no challenge for him.'

There was utter silence while the judge pondered over his notes and finally looked up and addressed the conflicting parties,'The court grants 2 weeks to the prosecution to gather evidence. The court grants bail to the accused on a security of Rupees ten lakhs and on condition that Mr. Mahavir Batra must be present for all hearings and does not leave the country. Case adjourned!'

Pandemonium broke in the courtroom. While the judge retired to his chamber, the press reporters rushed out to prepare their notes and the general public trudged out dejected at the proceedings.

'Thank you advocate ji. 'I genuinely meant it.'

'Mr. Batra this is surely a relief but do not forget that the case has a long way to go and the uncertainties will be countless. I will call you in a couple of days for a meeting in my office. Now I must rush as I have another matter to attend to.' Without looking at me, she rushed out of the courtroom.

From nowhere, Mukesh appeared and started slapping me and shouting, 'You murdering bastard, you killed my wife!'

Despite being a tall and robust Punjabi, I exercised self-restraint, refraining from unleashing my strength on the frail Jain gentleman before me. Exercising restraint, I yielded to good sense, and shortly after, the police stepped in, guiding me towards the awaiting jeep.

After signing certain documents, I was officially released and before I left, inspector Gawas commanded that I be present the day after tomorrow for questioning.

Chapter Eleven

Jatin Lal Singhal lounged in the balcony of his bedroom, savouring a steaming cup of morning tea. After 2 weeks of rain and overcast sky, he finally saw the blue with scattered clouds and wondered if he could see God and beg Him for the whereabouts of Paro in her heavenly abode, his daughter in law of whom he was very fond of. Thinking about her, his eyes brimmed. His thin lean body slumped on the chair in grief.

He did not believe the cock and bull story that his son Mukesh suspected of; her having an affair with his friend Mahavir who had just yesterday got the bail from court.

His mind could not conceive an iota of thought that his beloved daughter in law could ever have an extramarital affair with another man ultimately resulting in her demise by her alleged paramour.

He finally made up his mind and got up to have his shower, got dressed and calmly concluded his breakfast. His wife knew him well and quietly went about her routine and did not dare to ask her husband what was disturbing him.

Jatin Lal went to his bedroom, opened his wardrobe and with the help of a key he opened a concealed compartment and extracted ₹10 lacs and put them in his briefcase. Locking up the concealed compartment and taking along his briefcase he headed for the main door as his son Mukesh came out of his bedroom all dressed up for work and was surprised to see his father leaving for work.

'Papa I'll follow you a little later after having my breakfast.' Mukesh relayed the message to his father.

'You go ahead to the office, I have to go somewhere else for some work and will be in the office later on.' Without looking back, he left his apartment. He took the escalator for the basement. His chauffeur gave him a good morning salute and opened the car door for the boss to get in.

'Ranade, please head towards Juhu scheme,' In accordance with instructions, the driver steered the car to the left. On nearing the JVPS Police station Jatin Lal instructed the chauffeur to park the car and wait for him.

Entering the police station, he navigated his way to the office of the Station Head, Dy. SP Ramesh Mahatme. Speaking to the constable, he requested a meeting with the boss, offering his visiting card.

The constable went in and soon returned and opened the door for Singhal to enter.

Ramesh Mahatme looked curiously at the distinguished looking visitor and offered him a seat.

'Mahatme saab, I'm Jatin Lal Singhal - chairman of Office Necessities Pvt. Ltd. I'm also the father in Law of the unfortunate girl who was recently murdered and buried in the backyard of Mahavir Batra.'

Dy. SP. stood up and folded his hands in condolence and genuinely said,'I visited the morgue and looked at the body and let me tell you that as a policeman, I was deeply moved by the sight of the innocent girl and pondered on what wrongdoing such a seemingly virtuous person could commit to deserve such a tragic fate. Please accept my heartfelt sympathies to you and your family, especially to her husband, whose suffering is truly unimaginable.

'Dy. SP. Saab, I've come for a purpose and now after meeting you, I feel I'm sure you will help me out.'

'Tell me Mr. Singhal, how can I be of assistance?'

Singhal opened his briefcase and took out a newspaper wrapped bundle and offered it to Dy. SP then said,'Sir, this is ₹10 lacs towards Police welfare fund,(a terminology for bribe) I request that this case may kindly be handed over to CBI to quickly solve the case and the murderer apprehended, prosecuted and punished.' The police official kept the money in his drawer and said,'The decision can be taken by the Superintendent of Police, I will endorse the matter, and from that point onwards, you will need to pursue it further.

'Sure, I understand and will seek an appointment and do the needful.' Singhal shook hands and left the room.

On Sunday morning, as he read the newspaper after a breakfast that no longer brought him joy in the absence of his daughter-in-law, his mobile buzzed. Seeing the caller ID as 'Dy.

Sp. Mahatme', he greeted him with a simple "good morning" and took the call.

'Singhal ji, the SP sir has accepted my request and has delegated the case to Inspector Rasheed Inamdar, one of the finest in crime branch and he has solved some major tricky cases. So I'm glad the case has been delegated in the right hands.'

'Dy. Sp. Saab, I appreciate your assistance, and I'm truly grateful. Could you please inform me which station Rasheed Saab is affiliated with?'

'He is stationed at the main office at Worli, Google for more information and good luck to you sir.'

'Ranade, take me to the office.' Jatin Lal instructed his chauffeur.

On the way, his thoughts went towards his son and was a bit concerned that Mukesh's grief lasted just a week and now he seemed to behave his normal self, not that he was rejoicing but his body language was too casual but then he dismissed any kind of negative thoughts realising that the younger generation is less sensitive to sentiments and tend to move along in life unlike his generation which brooded over the loss of their loved ones for months at a stretch.

Back at the office, he immersed himself in the day to day business activities.

On Friday morning, he gave instructions to his chauffeur to take him to the CBI office at Worli towards the road leading to Mahalaxmi station along the racecourse tracks.

At the security checkpoint, he inquired about meeting Inspector Rasheed Inamdar.

"Do you have an appointment?" asked the security personnel.

'No I don't have one but you may kindly inform him that I am the father in law of the unfortunate lady murdered and buried in the backyard of the bungalow at Juhu'. The security repeated the information verbatim into the phone, and after a while, Jatin Lal was escorted by a policeman to the second floor. The officer knocked on a door.

"Enter!" called out someone from inside the room.

The door was pushed open and another policeman took over and led him to the table where a man in plain clothes sat.

Inspector Rasheed stood, his stout 6-foot-tall frame highlighted by arms resembling the legs of a robust 14-year-old boy. His upper body formed a distinct V-shape, tapering down to a narrow waist. His face chiselled with prominent jaws leading down to a broad chin which supported a deep cleft.

He gave the impression that if he walked, others would move aside to make way for him in respect. His face belied his physical self which exhumed a trustworthy and a gentle personality. Rasheed extended his hand and with a smile, shook hands with Singhal and sympathised with him for the loss of his daughter in law.

'So, sir what can I do for you?'

'Rasheed saab, I was very fond of my daughter in law, in fact she was more of a daughter to me.' Singhal removed his handkerchief and held it to his eyes because he was weeping and as a man of integrity, he would not like others to see tears running down his face.

Rasheed patiently did not disturb him. Later when his bout of emotion subsided, he wiped his eyes, blew his nose with a tissue and opened his eyes and looked at the inspector and said 'sorry.'

Rasheed consoled him,'I would have done the same thing, I understand your emotions.'

'The purpose of my coming to see you is that the case has been delegated to you and please don't mind my saying that normally there are many cases handled by individual officer so the investigation takes its own sweet time and during that time the accused is on bail and is enjoying his life and will continue till the trial is exhausted in all courts and finally lands in Supreme Court where it freezes for many years.' Jatin Lal Singhal opens his briefcase and takes out a bundle saying,

'Sir here is Rupees twenty lakhs for the Police welfare fund for just one reason and that is to try and solve this murder case as early as possible so that the murderer is put behind bars.'

'Mr. Singhal, under normal circumstances, I could have you arrested for attempting to bribe a law officer. However, I acknowledge your desperation that led you to make this offer. Please put the bundle back in your briefcase. I will do my best,

Jatin Lal Ji, I assure you," Rasheed stated. He stood up, signalling that the meeting was concluded. Jatin Lal Singhal also stood up, did a namaste, and exited the room.'

Rasheed sat down, folded his fingers under his chin with his elbows resting on his table and went through the conversation with Singhal. He had read the file twice and had the whole picture in the frame of his mind, quite a tricky and hard nut case to crack, but then he had to start working on some leads.

He summoned the constable guarding the office door and instructed him to fetch Sr. Sub inspectors Pramod Pandey and Santosh Moghe.

Within ten minutes there was a knock and both his trusted juniors entered and saluted.

'Take a seat!' Later, closing the file, he looked at both of them and asked,'Have you read the file I sent a couple of days ago about the murder and burial of one Mrs. Paro Singhal?'

'We have read the case but we're waiting for your instructions'. Pandey said.

'There seems to be many unanswered riddles, except that the circumstances under which the body was found and some sort of love triangle existed. Also the cause of death and approximate date and time have been established, so where do we start from.' Rasheed looked at the two for an answer who stayed mum, they knew their boss very well.

After a minute or two of silence he said,'Either the alleged murderer Mahavir, took out his car and drove to Singhal's apartment building and picked up Paro and brought her to his residence and due to some argument he murdered her. Since her husband's car and her personal car were both in the parking lot so I assume Mahavir picked her up, though I wonder what was the urgency especially when the weather was cyclonic and the whole of Mumbai was huddled in the shelter of their houses.' Rasheed surmises and then looks at both his juniors.

'I think sir, that first we should ascertain whether Mahavir actually picked up Paro.'

'And how do you intend to find that?'

'Firstly I will find out what cars Mahavir drives and then snoop around to find if anyone had seen the car on the fateful night.' Pandey said.

'Or I would check on various CCTV cameras installed between the houses of the victim and the murderer. CCTV would surely be on at Shoppers Stop, Juhu Gymkhana, Four star hotels on the way, JSW Marriott, the police post next to Gandhi statue at main beach and such others.' Santosh Moghe chipped in.

'All right, start with what we have discussed and in the meantime I will personally go and meet this murderer and find out what sort of man he is, okay dismissed.'

Inspector Rasheed declared, concluding the meeting with a determined gaze that hinted at an impending unravelling of the case.

As the door closed, Inspector Rasheed's eyes gleamed with a steely resolve, foreshadowing the twists and turns that awaited in the pursuit of justice.

Chapter Twelve

After being released from the police station, I hailed a taxi and reached my houseI settled the cab fare, and as I approached my house, the first thing that caught my eye was a red graffiti on the boundary wall, declaring 'HERE LIVES A MURDERER,' with red paint dripping beneath each ominous letter. Hastily, I entered my house and swiftly shut the door behind me.

The chilling message on the wall sent shivers down my spine, raising unsettling questions about what lurked in the shadows of my seemingly ordinary life. I hurriedly entered my house and swiftly shut the door, my senses on high alert, ready for the enigma that awaited within.

Once inside, I called a painting contractor who operated in Juhu to immediately paint the wall and offered him a handsome amount if he completes the job by evening. Next, I called the Security company and complained about the graffiti and instructed them to station two guards in the morning shift and two in the evening.

I filled up the bathtub with lukewarm water up to the brim, shed every piece of clothing I wore, and submerged myself in the tub. With my eyes shut, I revisited the days spent in judicial custody, a disconcerting echo of my existence now equated with petty thieves and thugs. Tears trickled down the sides of my eyes and soon spoke to my God as to why he brought this sad attack on my reputation and I wondered whether I would ever get out of this mess or will I have to rot in jail all my life.

I scrubbed my whole body with sandalwood soap and rinsed the tub. I repeated the process a second time and only then I felt that I have rid myself of the typical smell of a body which has not bathed for days.

I collected all the clothes and inner wear and stuffed them in the bin to be taken away by the garbage man the next morning.

Making a cup of coffee, I sat on the sofa, accompanied by two cracker biscuits. The initial call to the cook, instructing her to start coming from tomorrow, went unanswered. Subsequent attempts to contact the 'Jhadu pochha' maid also proved futile. It dawned on me that nobody would come near me, not even with a pole.

Realizing that, until I'm declared not guilty, my life would resemble that of a hermit, I contemplated why I should fret about the world. Armed with financial resources, I resolved to leverage that power to my advantage.

Engaging an agency that supplied part-time help for household chores, the necessary arrangements were set in motion without further ado.

'Hello is this Dependable Agency, I'm Mahavir speaking and I need a cook or a cleaning lady for my bungalow at Juhu.'

'Your name again, sir?'

'My name is Mahavir Batra.'

'Are you the same…..?'

'Yes I'm the same unfortunate person who is wrongly charged. Listen, to ease matters that since no female maid may work, I wouldn't mind male help and will pay handsomely.'

'Okay I'll have two of them ready and will call on your house in the evening and you can interview them. Do not talk about salary, just talk about work.'

With determination in my eyes, I proceeded to open the Samsung double door fridge. Methodically, I cleared its contents into a plastic bag, cleansing pots and plates to erase any lingering scent of stale food. In reality, there are no secrets; it's merely an effort to eliminate the lingering odour of leftover food and restore cleanliness to the house, neglected during my court or prison visits for my case. Yet, little did I anticipate that these seemingly routine tasks would intertwine with a more intricate narrative that awaited me in the corridors of justice.

Next, I wore a cricket cap and shut the door. I walked along the road and entered a grocery store and purchased essentials including milk, butter, bread etc. I then entered a cold storage shop and purchased fish, chicken and mutton and returned home by being careful of not having any eye contact with anybody on the road. I also saw men painting my boundary wall and wiping out the graffiti.

I helped myself to two fried eggs, some toasts and fried bacon with a strong cup of coffee.

I then lay on bed and within moments was fast asleep.

The persistent shrill of the door bell woke me up, I looked at my mobile and was surprised that I slept six straight hours. With squinted eyes I opened the front door. 'Sorry to disturb you, I'm from the Dependent Agency.'

'Come on in and bring the other two guys also and please shut the door. Take a seat and I'll just freshen up and be back.' The rep sat down while the two helpers stood.

I came back and sat down. First, I talked to the cook. He seemed sure of himself, dressed neatly, and could speak English, Hindi, and Garhwali. He listed all the dishes he could cook, covering everything in the Indian cooking menu. This raised my interest in knowing more about him. The other guy was equally smart and seemed confident of handling all household chores. I gave my acceptance and the rep instructed the two helps to wait outside the door.

'Sir for the cook ₹40000/- plus lunch and the other guy ₹30000/- monthly plus lunch. I didn't haggle since the Agency fee was included in the salary.

I seemed settled on the household front. The duo will start work tomorrow.

A shot in the dark, I buzzed Amita, the ringing continued but she didn't respond. I wondered why doesn't she delete my number. Sometimes I can't understand women psychology. She wants to hear my phone ringing but at the same time not to answer it.

Next, I phoned Babita and again the phone rang but it remained unanswered. I started wondering as to what will happen to my life, am I going to be untouchable until I'm proved 'not guilty' and even if I'm declared so then the praise will be showered on my advocate to have craftily argued my case to prove me innocent thus I still remain a murderer?

I looked up and spoke to God, 'Oh my revered God, on one hand you give me all the riches and on the other hand you take away all my Izzat, such a situation cannot be balanced, please help.'

In light of the challenges I'm facing, I've chosen to disregard the stigma and align my life accordingly. I've resolved to lead a regular life—tending to my business, attending court hearings, perhaps forming friendships, and building consensual relationships. Moreover, I've decided to embrace faith in God, acknowledging His blessings and recognizing this as a test of my devotion. With genuine love in my heart, I closed my eyes and offered a prayer.

There was one very important task to complete. Advocate Vandana had advised me to let go of some inheritance to my parents and brothers. If they file a civil case accusing me of manipulating and pressuring my grandpa into gifting me his wealth, it might influence my ongoing case. Such a civil case could potentially create a prejudiced perception, suggesting that I am not only a murderer but also a schemer.

It took me a lot of convincing and threatening of a long drawn civil trial that may last for 20 years and they may not be alive to hear the verdict, let alone losing the case.

Finally a gift agreement was prepared whereby my parents would be gifted certain properties and stock shares amounting to Rupees 12 Crores.

The gift would be sold immediately and Rupees 2 Crores given to each brother and the remaining Rupees 6 Crores for the parents. All legal papers were prepared by Mr. Seth and Adv. Vandana and the matter was wrapped up within two weeks.

Adv. Vandana congratulated me on clinching the deal. I used the usual tactic of inviting her for a dinner to celebrate which she refused point blank.

I started taking my business more seriously and picked up the nuances, finer points of retailing and some ideas about the working of car engines.

One fine day, as I was about to leave my Khar showroom, I stopped in my tracks when I saw a BMW 7 series stopped outside my showroom. A beautiful lady of around 25 years exited the car. She wore light blue slim fit jeans with a full length white Cotton shirt tucked into her jeans which seemed to be hanging onto her slim waist by the tightening of a broad light brown belt. The sleeves were folded up to her elbow, she wore dark sunglasses which she removed to face me with light brown eyes. She wore no wedding ring, her right wrist had a platinum bracelet and the left wore an Omega diamond studded watch.

The girl was very beautiful but behaved like an ordinary one with no airs about herself.

She was unsure whether I was a customer and so I took the lead and asked her,

'How can I help you madam?' I put on my best face and asked.

'My car keys don't seem to work sometimes. Also the horn on the left side is not working.' She replied in a British accent.

I took the keys from her and ignited the engines and pressed the horn which gave a funny farting sound. I pinched my nose and looked at her smilingly. She laughed embarrassingly and said in Hindi,'That's why I don't blow the horn.' We both laughed.

'Do you mind leaving the car here for a day? I'll take care of the necessary repairs or replacements and conduct a general checkup. This way, you can drive without any issues.'

She seemed to be making up her mind and so I said, 'I'm leaving for my other showroom at Bandra so if it's okay with you I can drop you if you stay close by.'

'I stay at 16th Road Khar Danda.' I called out to my chauffeur and he brought my car in front of the BMW and we both stepped into my Merc C Class.

Ramesh glided the car and joined the crowd and headed in the direction of Linking Road.

'Are you in India for vacation?' I asked, to strike a conversation.

'No, I've permanently returned to India. My parents sent me to the UK for pre-graduate and graduation, and now I'm a fully qualified psychiatrist.

'Oh that must be exciting, so are you opening a clinic?' I looked into her beautiful eyes.

'Yes I would love to, I've just been here for the last 15 days.' She did seem thrilled.

' Oh, let me introduce myself. I'm Mahavir.'

'I'm Seema Thakur.' We shook hands.

'Oh stop the car, that's the building I live in.'

'Once the car is ready I'll phone you if it's alright for you to share your mobile number?' She gave her phone details which I saved.

'Shall I send the car to pick you up so that you can drive away directly from the showroom?'

'That would be really nice of you.' There was an uneasy silence before she got out of the car and walked across the road and once on the pavement she looked across and gave me a genuine smile as she waved to me and entered the gates to her building.

I had a heavenly intuition that this was the girl with whom I would spend my life.

I also made a firm resolution that I will soon shift my residence from the bungalow. No girl will ever live in this house where a body was buried.

When I reached home, I pulled out the file pertaining to all the properties that my grandpa had leased. There were six of them, 3 at Nariman reclamation, 1 at Carmichael Road and one at Worli Sea Face. I fancied the Worli apartment. It is a 12 storey building with my apartment being a terrace flat with a great view and just 12 members owning apartments.

I got in touch with Mr. Seth who handled the collection of rent on a monthly basis and which was deposited into my Bank Account. My grandpa had infinite faith in Mr. Seth and I did not wish to disturb that arrangement. Of course, he was paid handsomely for his efforts.

The Worli apartment which was fully furnished was leased out to a senior member of some high commission of a Country and which was expiring in the next one month.

I informed Mr. Seth not to give further lease as I wished to shift into it. I explained to him the reason for the same, and he found it sensible.Also staying at Cuffe Parade would have been too far from my place of business.

THE INVESTIGATION

Chapter Thirteen

The next day, after leaving home inspector Rasheed Inamdar headed for Juhu and in an hour's time he stood outside the main door and rang the bell. After a few minutes' pause the door was opened by a man of fair complexion and as tall as Rasheed. He looked sad and dishevelled as if on the verge of ending life, Mahavir asked him what he wanted.

Rasheed told Mahavir his name and designation and that he was from the CBI.

Mahavir sarcastically told Rasheed that lately the whole of law enforcement has been coming and going so what difference will one more make? Mahavir opened the door and Rasheed walked in and seated himself on a single seater sofa and said that the case has been transferred to the CBI and his matter is delegated to him and so now on Mahavir will see more of him and his team of two who will soon approach him. Rasheed told him that he has read the report but he would like to hear from him.

'Tell me all that you want to say about the murder?'

Mahavir recounted the entire episode for what seemed like the umpteenth time, despite its brevity.

'So in a few sentences you have covered the murder of a woman.'

'I've said nothing about the murder as I do not know anything about it. I just told you about the discovery of the body, which is all that I know.' Mahavir clarified.

'By being silent you are harming yourself because once I know the truth I will come heavily on you and prepare the evidence in such a way that the judge will have no option but to give you the maximum punishment.' Rasheed ended his warning and looked menacingly at Mahavir.

'Sir I have a request but I'm afraid to spell it out because if you do not like or agree you will take any action.' Mahavir said to inspector Rasheed.

'Okay go ahead and speak freely.'

'Sir, I want you and your team to do everything in your power to nab the real murderer as early as possible. I am not asking any favour to spare me, you may continue investigating me also, but at the same time work on other angles. For this, I'm willing to pay you an incentive of Rupees thirty lakhs in advance. You have to find the real killer and if all your efforts fail then I will give you some leads which maybe helps you to nab the killer, though I'm not sure at the moment.' Mahavir said and looked at the inspector, not sure how he may react.

Inspector Rasheed appeared astonished by the proposition that the man before him was willing to offer an incentive to obtain evidence declaring himself a murderer. It left him questioning whether the man in front of him was the actual perpetrator or if someone else was involved.

With a deep sigh, Rasheed Inamdar got up and looked around the living room appreciating the furnishing and wall painting.

'I would like to have a look around your backyard garden.'

Mahavir took the lead, opening a spacious door that led to a meticulously curated garden. Vibrant flowers swayed gracefully in the gentle breeze.

'Which is the spot?' Rasheed looked at Mahavir who pointed towards the rows of flower pots. Rasheed looked around and sighted a spade. He moved a few pots and used the spade to dig and confirm the kind of mud and found it pretty loose and easy to dig.

They returned back to the living room and told Mahavir that his team members will approach him and to cooperate with them. As for the money offered, he said,

'If I had not committed that I would do nothing then I would have put you behind bars for bribery. Next time don't be so overconfident that it may lead you in trouble.' With those words, Rasheed walked out of the house, heading towards his waiting police car.

That night, as usual after dinner Rasheed would while away time listening to his two children jibbing and each trying to enforce his attention until the time comes to tell them to head for their room and go to sleep. He would then put on the tv and listen to some news until his wife comes out of the kitchen wiping perspiration off her face with her dupatta and head for the bedroom for a quick shower. Rasheed would then secure the main door, shut the lights and enter his bedroom after bolting from inside.

On the floor, his wife would say a brief prayer, expressing gratitude to God for a well-spent, trouble-free day. She would then join her husband on the bed. Rasheed was born and brought up on the Konkan coast around Vengurla. He was dark in complexion but his smart features and his height made him look attractive.

His wife Mumtaz was from Hyderabad, a beautiful woman with sharp thin nose, her wide eyes had jet black pupils surrounded by milk white cornea guarded by long eyelashes and her mane adorned with thick black tresses of waist length hair.

Rasheed kissed his wife and in slow motion got her rid of all her clothes and after a lengthy foreplay they finally copulated and later held on tightly to each other while they shuddered in final ecstasy.

Later, she would rest her head on her husband's chest as he engaged in light conversation. Often, he would realise that she had peacefully drifted into sleep.

Tonight, he captured her attention by recounting the events of the past few days.

He told her of the sensational murder of Paro and narrated his dilemma,

'A few days ago, the father in law of the victim came to my office and I could make out that the loss of his daughter in law had seriously affected his mind because he offered me a sum of Rupees twenty lakhs to hurry up with the investigation and put the culprit in jail.' He stopped talking and waited for his wife to comment.

'Paro must have been a very good daughter in law and the distraught father in law was furious, keen and curious to know as to what his daughter in law did to deserve murder and therefore avenge her loss. I doubt she would have an extra marital relationship with another man. Please don't be prejudiced by what I said.' 'Today, I went to the alleged murderer's house to get to know him and to see the site of the burial. The man is single, rich and good looking. During the talk he offered me Rupees thirty lakhs to find the true murderer. In simple words he requested me not to fabricate evidence so that his case is weakened for him and he loses the case in court, he doesn't know that I do not believe in such despicable acts.' Rasheed waited for his wife to comment.

'This man Mahavir is trying to put across to you that he didn't kill the lady in question, He could have said the opposite that he is offering you the money to water down all evidence so that he goes scot free. You are the policeman, my darling husband, so you solve the case because I'm tired and sleepy.'

Rasheed lay in bed with his eyes wide open in the darkness and felt elated that Mumtaz did not question him whether he had accepted the money offered, he shut his eyes and went to sleep.

Sub inspectors Pramod Pandey and Santosh Moghe stop the police jeep opposite Daria Mahal apartment building. The Secretary of the building waited for them to cross the road and welcomed them with a namaste, the two of them reciprocated similarly to the elderly gentleman. Pandey asked the secretary the positions of the CCTV who walked around and showed them. He told the secretary to get a copy of all the CCTV reels made by their security contractor for the last one month and will collect them the next day.

'How many security guards do you have at night?'

'We have two. Unfortunately both were absent on the night of the tragedy because of the storm. We have already furnished this information to the police.'

'The case is handed over to us in the CBI, so you will be seeing us more often. We still want to interrogate those two security guys. Please have them waiting when we come to collect the CCTV reels.'

'Sure I will make them wait,' the secretary confirmed.

'Any rumours floating around about that fateful night?' Moghe asked.

'Nothing really. It seems a real mystery as if the killer had predicted that it would be stormy and cyclonic the night he committed the murder. The world stayed indoors while the devil devoured his victim. Yes, one thing I need to mention is that Mrs. Murlidharan, a widow who stays alone on the first floor heard dogs barking ferociously who suddenly became silent, probably being served with food, she also heard the movement of the escalator at around midnight.' Moghe noted in his diary.

'How was Mrs. Paro Singhal, was she well known in this Society building?' Moghe probed.

'Well this is a high end society building and all keep to themselves but there was a collective decorum of courtesy towards other members and Mrs. Paro Singhal was no exception, she always smiled and greeted others.

The duo walked around the building keeping their eyes in vigil mode and noting down all that was relevant.

Together they sat in their car and instructed the driver to drive slowly below cruising speed towards the main Juhu beach.

They noted 22 spots having CCTV and decided to split between them and go through the reels in the next two days.

Their boss had instructed them not to interrogate the husband of the deceased, he would personally meet Mr. Mukesh and also visit his business establishment.

CBI inspector Rasheed Inamdar looked through the glass facade at the vast expanse of the Stationary outlet cum digital accessories situated on the ground floor of 'Merit' sky rise building in the hub of the financial nerve centre at Nariman Point. Rasheed was dwarfed by all the skyscrapers all around him.

Finally, with determination he went towards the entrance which opened automatically and entered the vast hall replicating a departmental showroom in a mall, the world of computers, mobiles, printers and various stationery were on display and being sold to customers by smart chick intellectual sales persons.

'Can I help you sir?' a salesgirl in navy blue trousers with a white shirt tucked in, distracted him.

'I've come to meet Mr. Jatin Bhai Singhal.'

'Do you have an appointment, sir?'

'No but just mention that Rasheed Inamdar wants to meet him.' The salesgirl departed reluctantly.

'Inspector saab, how nice of you to grace our business premises. Shall we go to my room and talk, the noise is overbearing over here?'

'Actually I've come to visit your son Mukesh.'

'Come I will take you to his cabin.'

'Jatin Bhai, I would like to meet him in private and discuss matters with him and also pay my condolences.'

'Sure, I understand.' He instructed the salesgirl to lead Mr. Rasheed accordingly.

Without knocking, the inspector entered the room and saw a gentleman with his legs resting on the side of his table top and laughing into the phone at some joke cracked by someone on the other side of the line. Mukesh noticed Rasheed and, setting his legs down and disconnecting the phone, stood up. He confronted the inspector, who was dressed in civilian clothes, and bluntly said,'Who are you and why did you enter my room without an appointment?'

'Sorry about that, though I met your father and he directed me to your office. I am inspector Rasheed Inamdar from CBI. I trust you are aware that the case of your wife's murder is now with us.' Rasheed noticed that the blood had drained off the face of the man standing opposite him.

'I'm sorry for being rude to you but my mood swings have become erratic and sometimes nasty after the passing away of my dear wife. Can I offer you a cup of tea or coffee?'

'No thanks. I've come for general questioning and not for any serious interrogation which may happen later.'

'Sure Inspector saab. After all, we need to nab the murderer and get him in jail as soon as possible.' Mukesh regained his composure and self confidence.

'Did you love your wife?'

"What a question to ask! Of course, I loved her, and she was the light of my life," Mukesh replied without hesitation.

'Was your wife in love with someone?'

'Well lately she showed some signs of being attracted to Mahavir, her murderer. We did have some arguments but she would scoff it off and vehemently deny it.'

'So, what were the signs that made you suspicious?' Rasheed looked intently at him and used all his experience and expertise to gauge Mukesh.

'She would take selfies with him in front of me. Once or twice, I observed their hands touching, and occasionally, she would visit Mahavir's house in the evening. Later, she would call me to join them for drinks while I'm on my way home from the office. He resides alone in the large bungalow; I hope you're aware of it," Mukesh added, feigning a sombre expression.

'Let me ask you point blank, did you kill your wife?' Rasheed probed and waited for a reaction. Instantly Mukesh shut his eyelashes thrice in succession and replied,

'How dare you insinuate against me! You have no right to make such accusations. I loved my wife very much,' Mukesh vehemently responded.

'Stay cool young man. I'm doing my duty to ask such questions formally and I've heard your negation and noted.' Rasheed scribbled in his diary to convince Mukesh.

'When did you notice that your wife was missing, what time was it?'

'I slept late after doing my office paperwork. That night was cyclonic with strong winds but I could hear my wife watching a movie on Netflix so I decided to sleep.

Early in the morning, I suddenly realised that my wife was not in bed by my side, I looked up the time, it was 6:00 am. I went round the apartment and when I couldn't find her, I panicked and knocked on my parent's bedroom door and woke them.'

'What time did you go to sleep?'

'Must be midnight,' Rasheed referred to his diary and said with a doubtful tone.

'The murder time is established around 11pm to midnight.'

'So maybe I slept around 11 AM after murdering my wife,' Mukesh said sarcastically.

'Be careful what you speak, I'm being patient, otherwise I carry an arrest warrant and can take you in judicial custody.' Rasheed warned.

'Sorry.' Mukesh reciprocated.

'Do you suspect that your wife may have clandestinely left by the main door to the waiting car of Mahavir who picked her up and took her to his house?'

'I suppose that's quite plausible and likely since my car was in my usual parking slot and both the keys were on the hook next to the door.'

'Both the keys?' Inspector Rasheed twisted his eyebrows and Mukesh realised the slip and immediately clarified, 'My key chain has a number of keys for the office door and filing cabinets. Her key ring just has the ignition key.'

Rasheed referred to his diary and looking straight at Mukesh, he declared, 'I need to inform you that as per medical reports the mortician certified that she had no sexual act before her death.' Mukesh just opened his jaw and looked like a dumb ass.

Inspector Rasheed Inamdar stood tall and, looking down at Mukesh, said, 'Can you hand over your mobile? It will be returned tomorrow.'

'But I need it for my business,' Mukesh protested.

'You will be informed of who called so that you may use the landline.'

Mukesh handed over the phone, after all the Jio phone given to him was returned back to Akhtar Kazi after the fateful night.

'Is there anything that you would like to disclose, now is the time. It will be a different ball game if I come across something that you should have told me.' Mukesh locked eyes with Rasheed and shook his head in disagreement.

Rasheed walked out of the office which was opened by a peon, walking a little further after the door was shut, the inspector turned around and beckoned the peon with his forefinger and once the peon was close to him, Rasheed showed him his police badge and told the peon to meet him outside during lunchtime and the peon gulped in his saliva in fear and shook his head in affirmative.

Ten minutes later some staff members came out for lunch followed by the peon who soon spotted Rasheed, the peon came over and Rasheed led him to a small Udupi restaurant serving veg thalis.

'What is your name?'

'Madhav Khare, saab!'

'Did you know Mrs. Mukesh?'

'Yes Sahib, she was a real Devi though she hardly came except to participate in auspicious pujas. It is very sad what happened to her.' Madhav said gravely.

'How about your boss, how is he?' Rasheed probed.

'He is proud, rude and very unpopular. His younger brother is a fine man like his father, the big sahib.' Rasheed prodded him further,

'Anything else you want to tell me?'

'One secret I want to tell you sahib.'

'Go on, tell me, I will do you a favour one day.'

'Mukesh sir is having an affair with Gayatri Mehta the chartered accountant of the Company. She is most of the time in Mukesh sahib's office. Once I saw them in an uncompromising situation when they were kissing and I opened the door and they did not notice me as I quickly shut the door.'

Rasheed paid the food bill and thanked the peon for his cooperation.

Back on his desk, happy with the day's proceedings, he wrote his report in a new file and replaced it in the file cabinet and while locking he saw his two assistants anxiously waiting for his attention.

'Sit and tell me.'

'Sir, there were 22 CCTV cameras installed along the route between the apartment building of the deceased and the alleged murderer's house. We split 11 each between us and our findings concluded with 13 cars travelling that route. We interrogated all the drivers and they all had irrefutable alibis especially on the horrific stormy night.' Pramod Pandey concluded.

'Sir there was also a delivery four wheeler carrier probably delivering milk.' Santosh Moghe chipped in.

'So did you cross check about the van?'

'No sir, we didn't find it necessary.' Sub inspector Pandey submitted sheepishly.

'In a murder case or for that matter the minutest detail may become the leading factor. Go back to where you started and trace the van movement and report to me. I'm giving you 2 days only!' The sub inspectors saluted and dispersed.

Chapter Fourteen

'Hello Seema ji, your car is ready. Would it be convenient for you to be picked up and taken to the showroom to collect the car? This is Mahavir calling.'

'Hi Mahavir I'm free and will wait for the car to arrive and yes I don't like ji etc. Just call me Seema.'

I laughed loudly. 'I'll be there in 15 minutes.'

I had goose bumps in excitement of meeting Seema. I instructed my chauffeur to take me to the same spot on Khar Danda Road.

She was waiting across the road; the most beautiful girl. She was wearing Khaki three fourth trousers with a Scottish chequered open shirt over a white neck less T-shirt tucked in. She acknowledged with a wave and crossed the road to enter the car, settling beside me. A subtle hint of Celine Dion perfume lingered, its mild essence enveloping her entire body with just a drop. She adorned small trinkets on the lobes of her well-shaped ears and chose not to wear lipstick, showcasing her naturally pink lips.

She pulled me out of my reverie by saying,'Hi Mahavir you haven't yet reciprocated to my Hi, for a moment I thought you were trying to remember who I am?' she sensed I was admiring her, because her cheeks responded by turning pink.

'Hi Seema, sorry for behaving like an ass, I was into some other thoughts.'

'Don't tell lies, you were admiring me, so nothing wrong in that, girls love it!' she gave a gurgling laugh. She quickly made me aware that she had been in the Western World for the last six years, where people express their emotions openly.

During the journey, she mentioned having explored some properties for establishing her consulting clinic but remained undecided due to her limited knowledge about the suitability of areas for business setup. She added that her father couldn't assist as he was too occupied.

The traffic was lean and soon we were at my service station. She saw the car well washed and sparkling. She used the key and sat on the seat and fired the engines and lightly blew the horn and was satisfied.

She paid the cashier and both faced each other as if preparing to say bye but unsure if they would meet again.

'It may sound brash but if I don't say then I may repent all my life. Will you have dinner with me on Saturday night?' I blurted and looked silly until she said, 'My parents are flying to Delhi to attend a marriage ceremony and I'll be alone with my brother. Most probably he will ditch me and be with his friends. So I suppose we can have dinner but we won't make it a late night.'

I controlled myself, all the staff and a few customers were watching us and so I hurriedly said, 'I'll phone you about the details,' I feigned officiously, a charade she picked up on. With an affirmative nod, she departed, and I rushed to my office, shut the door, and jubilantly danced a cha-cha-cha step.

She liked me and I was convinced so I did not try to preempt love at first sight. Though one day I would love to say that, 'I love you' and she telling me, similarly. My joy lasted for just a few moments, the mountain of a murder stigma glared down at me. I imagined a leopard sitting across me flicking its tail with the mouth open and staring at me. I shook my head vigorously to get rid of the imagination.

Once again I looked up and pleaded to God to somehow help me to get rid of my agony. Yes, if I had actually done the wrong then I must be punished. No amount of yelling to the world that I did not commit any crime will be entertained. I am the murderer and the matter is in court and only the court will decide whether I'm guilty, the verdict will only be decided on evidence and it cannot be denied that a body was found buried in my backyard.

I seriously contemplated not getting in touch with Seema. I had already inadvertently mentally hurt Amita, including some friends and all my relatives near and distant and it may take a long time for Seema to forget that she once loved a murderer. She looked too innocent, who gave the impression of blindly trusting the world at large, I just cannot hurt her whether she becomes mine or not.

I started crying in a semi drunken stupor. I had nearly consumed half a bottle. I suddenly remembered my grandpa who used to always say that if you are sincere and innocent and if you are falsely in troubled waters, God will bail you out through a living medium, God is merciful, face this treacherous world by keeping in mind that God is standing as a mountain behind you.

With a reassuring memory of my grandpa I felt lighter and suddenly realised that I was hungry and there was nothing except some frozen processed meat, stale hardened bread which I heated on a pan and applied butter and a slice of cheese. I filled a glass of cold 'long life' milk and gingerly took it to the table and munched away the sandwich chasing it with cold milk and then within minutes I was fast asleep.

Sometime during the night, I dreamt of walking on the Juhu beach with my grandparents and all three of us laughing.

We sat on the beachside restaurant of JW Marriott at Juhu, the sun had just set and the sky was luminous with orange and red hues and soon dusk slowly engulfed and transformed the day into night and the sky gradually showed the spectacle of twinkling stars. We were both mesmerised by watching the transformation.

A waiter approached our table and lit a candle and covered it with a glass frame to shield the flame from the light wind.

Seema's face glowed in the candlelight as she looked at me giving me a smile and said, 'How did you think of this beautiful place, Mahavir?' She said my name in an incredibly singing manner. She would stress on the 'Maha' and extend the 'Veer'.

'Oh! Mumbai is full of great destinations for good food and music but today being our first outing, I thought it appropriate to select a quiet and cosy surrounding so that we can talk and know one another and enjoy our conversation.'

Seema acknowledged my reasoning. She looked up in the sky, her long neck craning all around as if counting the stars, she looked at the gentle post monsoon waves crashing on the beach and receding into the folds of the mighty Arabian Sea. She watched couples walking on the beach holding hands. She finally smiled and looked at me as if reassuring herself that she made the right decision to accept my invitation.

I ordered the best white wine on the list. Seema stopped the steward from pouring more than a quarter of her crystal stem glass, we cheered and I noticed that she hesitatingly took a small sip as if fearing she may get drunk. I laughed throatily and assured her that wine taken in limited quantities has nearly no effect, putting her at ease.

'Tell me about you and your family.' I asked her.

'We are a standard four member Punjabi family: mother, father, boy and a girl. I studied in Scindia School in Gwalior and my brother studied at Doon.'

In general, she gave me an impression of a God fearing, well educated and conventionally career minded family. She narrated the life in a boarding school and how she now has a bunch of good friends who are in touch with each other.

'And how were your six years at Oxford?'

'My subjects were tough and required many hours of studying. London is a beautiful city but somehow I could not gel with youth of my age. Of course, I did have some good British friends.' She concluded.

'What about Boys, did you mix around with them?'

' You are asking if I went out on a date?' She laughed.

'I didn't date for the simple reason that over there in general, if a boy takes you out on a date, he feels it's his right to kiss and what not. No, I stayed away from dating.' She saw her wine glass empty and she looked around and soon a waiter appeared and lifted the bottle from the bucket to pour but Seema stopped him.

'Would you like something else to drink?' I asked, a bit concerned, eager to ensure her comfort during our time together.

'Yes, I'm feeling dry in my throat, can I please have some fresh apple juice?'

Soon dinner was served, consisting of piping hot crab meat in butter garlic sauce, prawns marinara spaghetti, and mushrooms along with a bowl of mixed greens. The dinner ended with orange soufflé shared between the two of us.

'Would you like to go on the beach for a walk? We'll walk towards the main snack shops closer to where the crowd is.'

'Sure, let's walk and spend some more time because all evening I've been talking about myself so now let's hear about you.'

We walked down the steps and after removing our footwear, it was gratifying walking barefoot on the cool sand.

I told Seema that I was the youngest of the six siblings of working parents, I told her that my father was a senior Banker and vaguely mentioned my school days and avoided telling her of growing up as an unloved and unwanted child. I did not even mention her relationship with my grandparents. She did not ask nor did I tell her where I lived.

I suddenly became quiet and silently we walked in each other's company. I felt guilty and miserable walking next to this heavenly girl. I needed to give her some inkling about my troubles so that when she actually comes to know of my matter she should not get totally surprised and disappointed that I turned out to be a fake and so I told her my matter as if the same had happened to a friend of mine.

I spoke, 'I have a very close friend who has landed in trouble,'

I began narrating my story, recounting every detail up to the point of him securing bail and subsequently being disowned by family, friends, and relatives. I emphasised that the case might extend for years, and until proven not guilty, he would be labelled a murderer. Even if the case is won, the credit would go to the lawyer, but the stigma of being a murderer would persist unless the police apprehend the real killer and the case is dropped.

Seema's face contorted in hurt and agony, and she responded with genuine concern, 'I'm truly sorry for your friend, whose life seems to have been ruined for no reason of his own. If he needs psychiatric advice, I'm willing to help.'

Her concern touched me, and I suddenly wanted to give this kind girl a hug. But, I stopped myself, and the feeling went away.

I also realised that it was a matter of time and she would know the truth. So instead of meeting her often and strengthening our relationship, it would be wise to lay off so that her hurt is minimal.

'Seema, I won't be seeing you for a month as I'm leaving for Germany for training.

Mercedes is coming out with a sophisticated model and I have accepted their training course.'

'Oh, what a shame, we had just started getting friendly and you are off and away from me. Mahavir, I really like you and will anxiously wait for your return.' She audibly whispered with a sad tone.

I summoned my chauffeur and sat in the car, dusting my feet and putting on my footwear. Driving towards the direction of Khar, we passed my bungalow and I dared not look at it but straight ahead.

THE INVESTIGATION

Chapter Fifteen

Sub-Inspectors Pramod Pandey and Santosh Moghe huddled together in the office, reviewing all the CCTV reels that traced the route of the white four-wheeler carrier tempo from Darya Mahal Apartments to Gandhi Ji statue at Juhu main beach. Beyond that point, there were no CCTV cameras along the route to Mahavir's bungalow, covering a distance of about 500 metres.

The time on the CCTV reel at the Statue showed 11.40 PM.

The two sub inspectors also noticed that the number plates in the front and back were rusted and not readable. The two of them concentrated minutely and finally managed to recognise the last two numbers as 66 or 68 on the back licence plate of the four wheeler. They phoned their boss and soon Inspector Rasheed joined them and after 5 minutes Rasheed was sure that the number plates had been purposely obscured to avoid recognition.

'I think black grease has been applied that will not get washed away in rain and later after their purpose is accomplished, the grease can be wiped off with a cloth soaked in petrol.' The inspector surmised and looked at his two assistants.

'Get back to tracking this four-wheeler and continue following its route on at least a few CCTV cameras, which may finally lead to their destination. Good work, boys,' the boss said as he walked away.

At sharp 6 o'clock, Rasheed Inamdar waited outside the Singhal Showroom and patiently stood watching the massive entry/exit door and finally he was rewarded by seeing the subsequent exit of Miss Gayatri walking out with sunglasses and heading towards the public paid parking area diagonally opposite the showroom. As she reached her car, Rasheed, who was just behind her, called, 'Miss Gayatri!'

'Yes please?' Her wrinkles on her forehead knotted in exasperation. Inspector Rasheed showed his police badge.

'What do you want?' Her fear or irritation was well camouflaged behind big framed glasses but the Adam's apple on her throat kept bobbing up and down.

'I need to ask a few questions regarding the unfortunate murder of Mrs. Paro Singhal.' Gayatri flinched.

'I read in the papers that the culprit is already apprehended, so how can I be of any help?'

'The accused is granted bail and so now we are collecting evidence by looking in all directions and making our case watertight.'

'But where do I fit in, I'm just an employee?' Gayatri said in a concerned and desperate manner.

'Miss, there's a restaurant close by, can you spare a few minutes so that we can peacefully converse instead of standing on the road and creating a spectacle of us?' Rasheed said politely, but in an authoritative manner. She followed him and soon entered a decent restaurant. They headed towards the corner table and Rasheed ordered two cups of cafe latte.

I won't make you wait till the order is served so let me put forward some questions,'How long have you been working in this firm?'

'Six years.'

'Whom do you directly report to?'

'To Mukesh, sorry Mr. Mukesh.'

'So all accounts are handled by Mukesh?'

'Yes. Though finally Mr. Mukesh is to report to his father.'

'Are you in a relationship with Mukesh?'

'What nonsense are you talking Inspector? I suggest you mind your language or I'm putting an end to this conversation and leaving!' Gayatri fumed, looking angrily at inspector Rasheed who gave a broad smile and said,'In that case, I'll have to call you to the CBI office for questioning, moreover now you cannot afford to t behave saintly, because the whole staff knows about your affair with Mukesh.' The blood drained off her face but she kept quiet.

'Did Mrs. Paro know about your affair?'

'I suppose Mukesh can answer this question! One thing I know for sure was, whenever Paro visited the office, she spoke very cordially to me. Frankly she was a fine lady and I do feel guilty at times.' Rasheed realised that this woman is smart and extracting true information may not be that easy.

'Were you and Mukesh in love or was it just physical?' Rasheed probed and tactfully awaited her reply.

'It was more physical.'

'So you never pressured Mukesh to divorce his wife?'

'No, never! I wouldn't like to hurt his beautiful and simple wife.' Gayatri lied. Rasheed took a deep breath and got up, thus ending the questioning and finding it hopeless to continue with this cunning lady.

On the way to the office, Rasheed Inamdar was confused and wondered as to where the case was heading and which direction to head. He couldn't figure out the motive for any of the key members.

Reviewing his questioning of each person, he concluded that…

1. Paro Singhal was an astute woman and would not fall prey to the charms of Mahavir who was handsome, rich and well mannered.

2. Mukesh had a physical relationship with Gayatri and nothing beyond. The Singhal family was an orthodox Jain Family and Jatin Bhai Singhal will never allow a divorce in his family. Mukesh would be aware that any such controversial act would bar him from family affairs and lead to detachment from the business as well.

3. Inspector Rasheed was aware that Mahavir was soon going to be married to Amita Bhatnagar who belonged to an army family. The possibility of a love triangle taking place was remote.

4. The inspector pondered about the elusive motive and the potential beneficiary of Paro's murder, lingering thoughts that troubled his mind. However, as the car arrived at his office building, he briskly disembarked and swiftly made his way to his cabin, where he promptly summoned his two assistants.

Sub inspectors Pramod Pandey and Santosh Moghe sat opposite their boss and patiently waited until he had written his report and had put the file back in the filing cabinet. Inspector Rasheed looked up and asked Pandey to speak.

'As mentioned earlier, we lost track of the Tempo carrier after the Mahatma Gandhi statue but continued our search, exploring whether it retraced its path or proceeded forward.. We were finally rewarded by sighting that same carrier at the corner road opposite the Santa Cruz Masjid moving towards the Hindu crematorium. The vehicle took a right turn to enter the small lane leading to SV Road at which point we again lost track.'

Sub inspector Moghe took over and said,'We analysed that there were three directions that the carrier can take after SV Road. Either towards Andheri, or towards Bandra or who knows it could cross the Milan railway underpass? Tracking the three directions will require manpower and for that we need your sanction and provision.'

'I will talk to my boss and get permission. My only worry is that we are not on a wild goose chase? However I'm sure that since you fellows have requisitioned, it means I must adhere to your request.'

Inspector Rasheed Inamdar rose from his chair, instructing the two to wait. He ascended to the third floor and, after a knock and salute, spoke to Dy. Sp. Pawar. He provided an update on the case's progress, as he regularly did, and requested additional personnel for two days. Dy. Sp. Pawar, who always trusted Rasheed, promptly sanctioned his request.

'Twenty men are sanctioned for two days so make the best use of them and remember I want results, don't let me down, good luck and all the best!'

Success is not final, failure is not fatal: It is the courage to continue that counts." - Winston S. Churchill. With these words, Inspector Rasheed Inamdar set forth his journey into the heart of the investigation. Little did he know, the pursuit of justice held more twists and turns than anticipated.

Chapter Sixteen

"Tring Tring," my phone shrieked.

I answered the phone to find Seema calling. It had been 15 days, and my patience to remain silent was waning. Inwardly, I was dying to hear her voice, but I was determined never to hurt her.

Life plays truant with us humans. Sometimes I wonder why our life is a roller coaster ride, why the ups and downs and a straight line as seen on a monitor screen in ICU when you are dead?

I remembered my grandfather discussing the roller coaster of life.

He said to me, 'Putr, I struggled after marriage, working as a mechanic and raising three children in the early days of my married life. My prayers were answered when the owner of the shop retired and I bought the shop on instalments. After that, I never looked back,and took risks and soon I had three service stations. I loved my God and he showered me with his blessings. Never ask anything from God, just pray and ask for his blessings and that will get you what you desire.'

I had my legs rested on the side of my table top and with closed eyes I was thinking of the words of wisdom that grandpa uttered and suddenly I heard the clearing of the throat and was surprised to see Seema sitting opposite to me.

'So how come you are back from Germany in just a fortnight, was the training not worth it or you missed your country?' Seema was wearing a churidar set with white kameez and bottle green churidar and a white and green shaded Dupatta. A black bindi was all the makeup she wore. She kept staring at me and waited for me to respond. I stayed Mum. She continued,

'I missed you Mahavir, if you had returned back cutting short your trip, didn't you feel like calling me?' Seema spoke as if hurt.

'Seema, let's be honest here. It's better if we don't meet. I fear that our continued meetings might lead to a deeper connection, and I don't want to see you sad or hurt. I'm just not the right person for you,' I expressed sincerely.

'But you are not being honest. You need to spell out the reason why we should not be meeting? I mean, what are you talking about?'

'You will come to know soon and then you will thank your stars. The scars of our friendship will then sentimentally fade away.' Riddled with guilt over dampening the spirits of this wonderful girl, I resolved to stand up and depart before I succumbed to my emotions. Despite my intention, Seema remained unfazed and somewhat commanded me to take a seat.

'You want to break up with me because of the story of your friend that you mentioned to me? Now you listen to me. I carry an intelligent head on my shoulders and I blindly don't do things. After our last meeting, I mentioned your name to my brother and it was weird to see his temper and immediately, he asked me to google your name and I did and everything tumbled out.'

She glared at me and continued, 'The next day, I visited The Times Of India dealer and got home a heap of newspapers and for the next four days I read all that was mentioned about the murder, burial, custody and bail.' Tears started running down Seema's cheek. I didn't move to console her, I just wanted to break free and let this darling of a girl forget an unpleasant incident. I remained silent.

'Speak up my dear, you have no one by your side except me and I am convinced that you had no part to play in this unfortunate murder and have been framed for being a soft target, maybe I can help you out but I need to have your complete faith to trust me.'

'On one condition that you will not emotionally get involved with me!' I insisted.

'Naturally yes, I do not want to be emotionally associated with a man who has a stigma of being a murderer.' Seema threatened.

'Can you kindly phone Inspector Inamdar that I seek an appointment with him?'

'To discuss what?'

'I'll let you know later, I'm just working on a hunch, I am not sure of the results.' Seema clarified.

'Can we have dinner tomorrow night?' I'm truly flabbergasted by this lovely girl. A few moments ago she was threatening me and now she wants to have dinner with me. I give in and agree to have dinner.

By now, I had followed a routine of my own to conduct my life. Mornings on the beach, two visits to my three workshops, all meals at home. Two pegs of single malt while watching a movie on Netflix.

I had many interrogations with Inspector Inamdar and I would answer the same questions repeatedly. Possibly trying to catch me off guard and giving an answer not in consonant with the earlier questioning. I kept telling the truth and that is all that I would do.

I sat in the lobby facing the Entry of the Taj Lands End Hotel at Bandra sea face and waited.

Many heads turned towards the entry door when Seema breezed in with her hair flying due to the air curtain and soon having spotted me she confidently started walking towards me.

Tonight, she had a thin film of lipstick covering her lips and as usual delicate trinkets swinging at her ear lobes. She wore a sleeveless black evening dress that ended four inches above her knees exhibiting fine muscled calf which were emphasised due to her stiletto sandals. I dared not look or gaze at her chest region.

We took the escalator to the roof garden and sat at our reserved table close to the railings, overlooking the sea. It was nearing new moon night, meaning that the moon would soon set and the night would be dark, though mildly illuminated by the stars but would not be a match to the brilliance of the moon.

'So what type of dinner would you like to have, accordingly we can then order our drink.' I asked.

'I would love North Indian food, I'm crazy for it. Especially the black daal with slightly crisp tandoori roti.' Seema said with excitement just like a teenager, I just adored her at that moment.

'That's all? What about chicken boti kebabs and maybe an aloo gobhi, Punjabi style?'

'Then I won't have space for a kheer or phirni as desserts?' She declared, childishly.

'Do you want some red wine?' She refused a drink and sipped some bottled water.

'Do you mind if I have a scotch for myself?'

'Not at all, go ahead please.' Seema urged.

'So how do you pass your time, I'm totally getting bored? Sometimes I wonder what life is all about.' She audibly pondered, a bit frustratingly.

'That's not a very encouraging utterance from a bubbly girl like you. Tell me what's not going well or as per your expectations. Let me be your psychiatrist temporarily.' I guffawed and encouraged her to speak.

My drink arrived and I took a big satisfying gulp and looked at her, expectantly.

'Well, nothing seems to be going right. I'm unable to find or choose a good location for my consultation clinic. I have no friends, I lost them all after I went abroad for studies, I tried to revive meeting some school mates but soon realised that they would snigger behind my back, making fun of my accent. I'm trying my best to get back to speaking English the Indian way but it will take some time. The next thing is you. I was happy that I now have a great male friend only to learn that you are involved in a murder case. Though I am convinced, hopefully right, that you are innocent but that iota of doubt keeps lingering behind my head. So you realise the uncertainties happening to me.' Her eyes brimmed but being a brave girl she did not allow a droplet to run down her cheeks. At that moment I felt a strong urge to hug her and say a few words to comfort her but resisted. I realised she didn't want sympathy neither should I think of her as a weak sentimental girl. I stayed silent. After a few moments of silence, I spoke.

'You should set up shop in a polyclinic building which has consulting clinics for general physicians, physiotherapists, eye clinic, urologists, nephrologist and including other streams connected with human anatomy. It will then become easy for you to approach them since you have now become their neighbour and a psychiatrist is essential for various types of patients that include patients recovering from a cancer operation, life threatening ailments, a widower. I mean you know better what sort of patient will approach you or are recommended to you by doctors. So I know a real estate agent and will get back to you in a day or two.' Seema seemed relaxed and I continued.

'Now talking about friends, gone are the days when there were good friends who only thought good about you and felt sad if something wrong happens to you and if possible help you out.

In present times, we are all selfish. We want friends to party, we want friends to have lunch together and be in the company of friends to joke and laugh about and of course to gossip, there is no sentiment attached. It will be better to get back to your school friends and be honest to them about your accent and that you are trying your best. Invite them to a restaurant to celebrate your birthday and gradually win their hearts.'

'You seem to be giving me psychiatric treatment.' She said in a lighter tone.

'Doctors also consult another doctor when he is sick.' I answered in a logical way, she understood as to what I implied.

'Now about me. I am sure you must have been very distraught when you learnt about me. For a few moments it may have shattered your feelings. I promise you that I'm deeply concerned and distraught at the turn of events in my life. Especially after losing Amita's love. And just when I thought I'm free of emotions for being disowned by her, a beautiful and lovely girl who is presently sitting opposite me, enters my life. I agree not emotionally but definitely forming an impact on my turmoiled frame of mind and so thought of ending our friendship as mentioned earlier.' I looked intently for her reaction which was none, non committal, I took a mouthful of my second drink and continued,

'You see Seema, nobody can help me, neither God nor my friends and well wishers, not even the judge or even you. Only the police can help by apprehending the culprit with indisputable evidence whereby the killer is forced to surrender. Until then, God wants me to suffer.' Now I could see teardrops running down her cheeks. I pull out a freshly laundered handkerchief for her to wipe her cheeks and dry her eyes.

'Your kerchief has a nice fragrance of the aftershave you used,' she smiled and lightened the environment around us.

'Seriously Mahavir, I know your matter and I think I can be of some assistance.' Seema said with confidence.

'How can you be of help? I doubt if your academic course taught you how to catch murderers.' I chided her.

'Just arrange an appointment for me to meet inspector Rasheed Inamdar and please do not ask me why or for what reason. Will you arrange the meeting?' She asked in a desperate manner.

'I'll do my best but will not be liable if he refuses to meet you, agreed? I questioned her.

'Agreed!' Seema committed.

She had consumed a full plate of sweet phirni and I enjoyed watching her consuming it delightfully like a little girl.

I dropped her off at her apartment building, and she again reminded me about the inspector.

THE INVESTIGATION

Chapter Seventeen

The inspector strode briskly to his office, maintaining a quick pace. Once inside, he refreshed himself, reaching for the neatly folded towel that his wife, Mumtaz, had thoughtfully placed in his lunch bag. As part of his routine, he reciprocated by returning the towel to the lunch bag before heading home, a simple yet intimate ritual.

The constable opened the office door, gave a crisp salute to his boss and announced that a lady was waiting to see him and that she says she has a prior appointment.

'Yes, send her in.' He remembered the call that he received from the accused Mahavir.

He was extracting Mahavir's file from the cabinet when he heard the clearing of throat. He turned around and was surprised to see an extraordinarily beautiful looking girl with an intelligent forehead with nearly straight eyebrows over large eyes with long curved eyelashes. He distracted himself and offered her a chair while saying,

'I'll be with you in a minute.' He removed the file marked in bold letters, MURDER FILE OF MRS. PARO SINGHAL. In the left hand bottom it was marked with a black felt pen, 'Accused Mahavir Batra'.

Rasheed put the file in front of his chair, sat down and looked up at the good looking girl. He opened his 6 inch diary and with a pen in hand asked,'How long have you been acquainted with Mahavir?'

'Just a month and a half, more or less.' Seema confidently replied.

'Did you strike your friendship with Mahavir before or after the murder of Mrs. Paro Singhal?'

'After!' Seema looked straight in his eyes and replied.

'When did you come to know that he was accused in the murder of Mrs. Paro with whom he was having an affair.' Rasheed never liked mincing words. He was straight forward and expected answers to be straight forward also.

'About a month after we met, we had gone out for dinner a couple of times.' Seema replied as a matter of fact. Inspector Rasheed was appalled at the true grit of this girl.

'After you came to know about his involvement in a murder case you still maintained and pursued your friendship with this man in question.' Rasheed raised his voice a bit.

'Yes.' Seema replied defiantly.

'Are you in love with this man, are you crazy, do your parents know about all this?' Rasheed boomed.

'At the moment I'm not in love with him but I find him an interesting man. I cannot say now, that our friendship will turn into a love affair and yes my brother knows about it and very soon I will mention it to my parents.'

Rasheed was now getting impatient and desperate to put some sense in this foolish girl.

'He has ditched his fiancée, a Miss Amita and then Mrs. Paro and now you, he is conniving and has the art to bring girls under his spell. Inspector Rasheed cautioned.

'I am aware of everything including what you think you have disclosed and in spite of all, I would say that Mahavir is innocent.' Seema coolly uttered at the bewildered man sitting opposite.

'How do you know everything? Rasheed asked with irritation written on his face.

'Because Mahavir told me everything and let me tell you that he has a strong alibi which he has not disclosed because it might cause distress to a particular individual, something he wishes to avoid.' Seema was now breathing heavily due to strenuous conversation.

'So you believed all the cock and bull story that he narrated to you and you believed all his bullshit that he said to impress you.' The inspector let out a laugh.

'Inspector saab, I've done my Masters in Psychology from the UK and I stood first and was a gold medalist. I'm a trained psychiatrist and can interpret human sentiments. I have done a lot of questioning with Mahavir and I find that he has no motive or reason to kill Mrs. Paro.' Rasheed was stunned at this disclosure and now he looks up at Seema with a certain kind of respect.

'You are no one to tell us whether Mahavir is guilty or not, leave that to us policemen who have solved hundreds of cases. So now miss Seema, for what reason you wanted to see me, please mention quickly as there is loads of work for me to do.'

'I request a session of hypnotic psychoanalysis on Mr. Mukesh Singhal which will give the insight of his unconscious mental process that is sometimes described as 'Depth psychology'. This kind of psychological method was adapted by physiologist Josef Breuer, an Austrian.

The test may not be 100% accurate but it will give a trend that a patient adopts to whether he is telling the truth or not.' Seema looked keenly at the inspector whether he understood what she said.

'The results of such tests are not admissible in court and secondly such tests require the permission of the presiding judge which is generally not given.' Rasheed clarified.

'We could find some other way whereby he volunteers for the test.' Seema insisted.

'But why do you want to conduct the tests on him?' Inspector Rasheed was curious.

'Because Mukesh has a motive. His lust for that woman Gayatri supersedes his mental awareness, I may be wrong in my assessment but there is no harm in trying it out.'

'Where did you meet Gayatri and how do you know about her?'

'I never met her, but Mahavir tells me that he met her at a couple of parties and noticed Mukesh and Gayatri whispering and sometimes arguing. Mahavir describes her as a sex bomb.'

Give me a day, let me work on it and will call you accordingly.' The inspector assured her.

Seema walked out of Rasheed's office leaving him in deep thoughts.

It was nearing the end of monsoons, Inspector Rasheed ran across the pavement to escape the light drizzle and the security guard at the automatic door of Office Essentials' saluted Rasheed who was now aware about the inspector. Rasheed nodded at the guard in acknowledgment and proceeded towards Mr. Singhal's office cabin. As a courtesy, he asked the peon to inform his boss of his arrival.

Singhal himself walked to the door and invited the inspector to enter. Over a cup of tea, they exchanged pleasantries before Singhal patiently awaited Rasheed to articulate the reason for his visit.

'Singhal saab, I need to ask you a favour, it's not really a pleasant favour but with more developments cropping up, I have to eliminate a certain number of individuals from the list of suspects by satisfying myself that they are not involved. To achieve this, I am employing various interrogation methods.'

Inspector Inamdar looked with uncertainty whether Singhal understood.

'I'm sorry inspector, I've not understood, please spell it out freely. After all, we are on the same side.' Rasheed audibly takes a deep breath and finally says, 'Singhal saab, I request you to convince your son to agree to doing a hypnotic psychoanalysis test, it's not a lie detector test but a general check up on the frame of mind.'

'Have you spoken to my son and did he disregard your request and most importantly I'm asking you that do you suspect my son's involvement in the murder of his wife? If so, then it is preposterous.'

'I also agree. That is why the test is carried out and I tick him off the list.' Rasheed lied convincingly.

Singhal rings the bell on his table and the peon immediately opens the door and is instructed to call Mukesh to his cabin.

'Yes papa.' Mukesh simultaneously sees Inspector Rasheed and stops in his tracks as if an invisible wall suddenly sprouted. Inspector Rasheed stood up and gave a reassuring smile and shook hands.

Senior Singhal explained to his son all about the visit of the inspector and sought his willingness to take the psychoanalysis test.

'Sorry papa I don't agree to undergo such ridiculous tests which should actually be done on various suspects rather than on me, as I was deeply in love with my wife, I may never get out of my grief, my life is ruined because of that bastard Mahavir.'

'You see we are required to satisfy and clear all doubts, it is the basic procedure of a crime investigation and that is why I'm requesting this test. It's not that you will not be in your senses, you will be aware of what you are saying. It's as simple as that.' Rasheed left his words trailing.

'I see no harm in accepting to have the test done, if you do not agree they can approach the court and get their permission and order.' Senior Singhal tried to convince his son.

Two days later, Mukesh entered the CBI building, was escorted to the lift and exited on the 4th floor and was made to sit in a square room. The room was especially rearranged by removing the wooden table and old chairs and instead a comfortable single seater sofa was placed and a straight chair opposite it.

A few moments later, inspector Rasheed Inamdar entered the room escorting a beautiful young girl.

'Mr. Mukesh, meet Dr. Seema Thakur, psychiatrist who will conduct the test.'

'I thought this young girl was a college student.'

'You are right I have just completed my post graduation and you are my first assignment.'

'You are very beautiful to be a doctor.' Seema ignored the comment and asked Mukesh if she could start.

Rasheed excused himself, leaving the room. Upon closing the door, he entered the adjacent room, where a TV monitor displayed Mukesh comfortably seated and relaxed. Seema, on the other hand, opened her file and sat with crossed legs. Ever so subtly, she swayed her upper body, causing the small pendant in her delicate necklace to pendulum. Mukesh's gaze soon followed the gentle swing.

Seema stretched her right hand and mildly caressed the mane of thick hair of Mukesh, saying,

'If you want, you may shut your eyes or you may keep looking at me.'

'I prefer looking at you, that is a beautiful pendant you are wearing, is it a topaz?'

Seema ignored the comment and asked him if he liked the silence.

'Yes the silence is bliss and I feel so comfortable talking and watching you.' Mukesh shut his eyes and smiled to himself as if he had entered a paradise. Seema did a thumb up sign indicating to Rasheed that Mukesh was now in a semi conscious trance.

'Did you love Paro?'

'Not really but I liked her as my wife because she was beautiful and sophisticated.'

'So why didn't you love her?'

'She was cold in bed and I had to take all the initiative for love making.'

'So she was not up to your mark like other sexy women that you saw around? For instance, like Gayatri from your office?' Seema was now entering dangerous waters.

'What has Gayatri got to do where my wife is concerned?'

'I appreciate that the two are different subjects but sometimes men have a secret fixture and adoration for another woman which has an effect on the conjugal relation with the wife.'

'Yes to some extent you may be right.' Mukesh concedes.

'Have you slept with Gayatri, have you made love to her?'

'How dare you ask such a question, don't bring Gayatri into all this, she will not like it if she comes to know about our talk.'

'So you are pretty close to her informally, more like friends though she is just an employee in your office.'

'Yes you can say that.'

'Since your wife is no more, would you marry Gayatri some day?

'Why do you ask irrelevant questions? Who knows about the future, what awaits you or me.'

A constable tiptoed a crumpled ball of paper and handed it to Seema. She read and put her palm to her mouth, a bit scared.

'Did you kill your wife Paro?' Seema looked scared and quickly stood up and waited.

Mukesh twisted his face and started crying and said loudly,

'Do I look like a murderer? Am I behaving like a murderer so why and why do you have the guts to ask such a ridiculous question?'

Mukesh opened his eyes and looked at Seema and glanced around the room and felt that his cheeks were wet. He sat up straight and said,

'It seems I went to sleep. He stood up and wiped his face, soon inspector Rasheed entered and took charge.

'Mr. Mukesh thank you for agreeing to take this test and let me tell you that you conducted yourself very well and you were totally honest in answering the questions. The constable will accompany you to the exit. Thank you," Rasheed said, shaking hands with Mukesh.

Seema and the inspector went down two floors and entered the Inspector's office and he ordered two cups of coffee.

'So tell me the results of your psychoanalysis test. He was in semi-trance and that is the reason he did not own up to anything but I'm sure your expertise can form some impression of his answers.'

'Mukesh is a very complex person, a kind of person with a split personality. He can impress some people and some may see through his facade and not like him at all. Now, to your question of what the test result is so I'll tell you but they are just guidelines to pursue. Such results are never 100% accurate, so here it goes.

1. Mukesh never loved his wife.

2. He is having a sexual relationship with Gayatri.

3. Generally he is a fake person carrying a bag full of hidden secrets.

4. He did not vehemently deny that he killed his wife. The tears that ran down his cheeks were the result of his subconscious guilt.

5.Lastly, I can say that he had some part to play in the murder of his wife.

'Please do not divert from your line of investigation, please continue accordingly without what I said influencing you.'

'Thank you Seema ji, I will keep an open mind and continue to investigate as before.' Seema stood up and after a courteous goodbye, she left the room leaving a lasting impression on Rasheed.

After the door was shut, Inspector Rasheed picked up the internal phone and spoke to sub inspector Pandey to come up along with sub inspector Santosh Moghe.

Rasheed signalled the two to sit and continued writing notes about the happenings of the last one hour and on finishing, he looked up pensively at his juniors and asked,

'So how are we moving in the Paro Singhal murder investigation?'

Pandey opted to speak first,

'We tracked the white Tempo carrier which crossed the Milan Subway and after crossing all the marble godowns the carrier joined the main highway and moved towards Jogeshwari Eastern suburb and there onwards we lost track. However we are sure that it turned left into one of the by lanes and moved towards the Western suburb. A couple of early morning revellers and a few restaurant workers confirmed having seen the carrier moving West between 4 AM and 4.30 AM.'

'So how do you want to proceed further?' Inspector Rasheed questioned the two who looked at each other as to what to answer their boss.

'See, there are two ways to tackle the matter. Our aim is to find the owner of the carrier. Either we approach the Transport Dept. and alphabetically check on the last two numbers i.e. numbers 66 or 68 or 88. Now the computer may point out close to 999 vehicles or I can seek permission from my boss to again sanction close to 50 field men this time and use them to spread all over West Jogeshwari and identify a white Tempo goods carrier having its last two numbers as 66, 68 or 88.' The two sub inspectors agreed whole heartedly.

'Sir one more matter, a middle aged couple stay on the 1st. Floor of the Singhal Apartment building towards the right while facing the building, in fact exactly in line with Singhal apartment above and while questioning him he mentioned that around 11.15 that night he heard a heavy vehicle start up and by the time he opened the balcony and looked down, he saw a goods carrier moving away outside their boundary wall. He couldn't make out the colour of the vehicle because he could not stand outside for more than ten seconds due to the strong winds. But the time is established.'

'Good work and will let you know about the field men once the boss sanctions it. Dismiss.'

Chapter Eighteen

I shifted from Juhu to the Worli sea face apartment on the 12th floor. It was a sprawling flat and I marvel at my grandpa having purchased this beautiful apartment. I sometimes wondered why he created such wealth in real estate by purchasing so many apartments. Was he not aware that he has to leave everything here when he dies? Maybe the circumstances were different when he was young and full of life to purchase a property for each of his family members so that they may live comfortably and who knew that real estate would boom to such an extent.

At some point, his well-intentioned dreams soured as he observed his son and grandchildren lacking love and respect for him and Grandma. It left him heartbroken, and perhaps, with me being the last, the entire family bunched us with my grandparents and eventually abandoned us.. It's pure Karma I realised while sitting in the balcony and admiring the clear cut horizon.

At that moment I thought of Seema, such a beautiful girl, her smiling face could bring joy to the saddest of humans. She was the type whom the cruellest of people would think twice to harm her.

My phone buzzed and I smiled,

'I was thinking about you, you know I wouldn't tell a lie.' It sounded so hollow with a murderer tag round my collar.

'I believe you because I was thinking about you. Can I come over, I just feel like sitting next to you silently.' Seema emphasised.

My eyes brimmed and I could feel myself being pulled into the vortex of sentiments.

'I suggest that let me send my chauffeur, he will pick you up and later drop you back. It's still early evening so by the time you arrive, it will be perfect for viewing the sunset.' I said.

'Listen! While I'm waiting for the car, I'll order some dinner and bring it along.'

'No, Worli sea face has many restaurants so we can have some hot dinner.' I suggested.

'When did you shift to Worli, you didn't mention earlier?'

'Just two days back, I can't stay at the Juhu bungalow; the sounds at night are too eerie and unsettling..'

'I agree, good decision but you also sound richly rich, we'll talk more when we meet.'

I had shifted with three bags of clothes and nothing else. There will be plenty of time to sort things out. One or two residents have recognised me and as far as possible they won't take the escalator if I'm also on it. Who cares?

I took a lengthy shower, hard rubbed my body and applied moisturiser on my under arms and on my leg joint area giving me a nice velvety feeling, I put my long legs into a baggy trouser with a flowery T-shirt and with my hair well groomed I looked in the mirror and felt cool, definitely not a murderer. Shit, the stigma. I shook my head vigorously to get rid of negative thoughts and went over to the music set and played some light symphony music and awaited the girl, the final girl to live with, when and if the time comes.

My thoughts went back to Amita and I did remember from time to time not for any craving but to wonder how the money factor was important to her. I especially remember the evening when for the first time I was invited for dinner at her house with her parents in attendance and how she made me disclose my wealth. Money is an important factor while marrying a boy, a sense of security must prevail, but during that dinner meeting she wanted to stress to her parents that she was marrying a rich man. I did not mind her not phoning me on being arrested, it is quite understandable, but once I was on bail and she did not try to get in touch with me was hurtful, after all if she was in love with me she should have shown concern. What if such a thing happened post my marriage, would she just ditch and run away from me. Anyways all happens for the good, my faith and indebtedness essentially to the Almighty God was infinite.

I have full faith that He will pull me out of the stranglehold that I was tied into and I strongly believe that it was his Will that I accidentally met Seema.

The doorbell chimed and I rushed towards the door and we gave a bright smile to each other.

'I was thinking about you.' I said.

'Sorry got a little late due to heavy traffic on the sea link,' she tactfully skirted my words. Also stop staring at me, it's bad manners.

'I was just admiring your dressing up, it's the first time I've seen you in jean short pants with a lovely choice of your black top'. I justified myself.

'I have some good news to tell you.' She said with excitement.

'I also have some good news, I'll tell you after you have said yours.' I smiled and said.

'As per your advice I've managed to find an impressive office space at a polyclinic building at Khar on the main road. I've given the contract to an interior designer to do up the place, I've also ordered a few instruments and gadgets required for my line of work. I think the consulting clinic will be ready in a month's time, I only hope I get patients.' Seema said worriedly.

'Can I seek to take an appointment as your first client?' I chided.

'Why, what's wrong with you?'

'Frankly nothing but at least I'll get the opportunity to lie on the consulting settee and be near you.' I said jokingly.

'Mahavir, please do not say any sentimental phrases, I do not want to fall into a situation until you are cleared of your charges. I mean I am sure you are innocent and that is why I'm sitting here but there are always the external forces doing their best to put you behind bars , so then where do I stand in life? I'm just holding on to a shoestring hoping it does not snap. So let us stay as good friends and hope things will straighten with time.' Seema made a sad face but convinced me philosophically. I looked up and prayed to free me of my problems so that I can hold this fine girl in my arms and keep on holding her all my life.

'Now tell me about your good news.' Seema was curious.

'Can I pour myself a drink and I've made some great sherbet for you, you'll love it.

'Okay fine, but I suggest we order food, I don't want a late night.' We ordered food that I know she loves.

'Yesterday was my date in court and I'm glad to state that the prosecutor asked for an adjournment, they have not been able to progress into the investigation for want of evidence, the police have asked for another 30 days which the honourable judge agreed, thus extending my bail. It's in the newspaper, do read it when you go home. I tapped on three newspaper dailies lying on the table.'

I went to pour a second drink but the doorbell chimed and hot dinner had arrived. Both of us transferred the contents in serving bowls and later poured in our individual plates. I loved seeing Seema attacking the butter chicken, dal tadka and wheat tandoori rotis. The food was from one of the best neighbourhood restaurants and to top it all was sweet phirni or what is known as Indian custard.

After dinner, we sat some more; admiring the yellow half moon which had crossed the zenith and was now in the setting mode. After spending a few moments at idle talk, Seema got up, picked her bag and the newspapers, and requested that I call it a night. Since it was just 10pm, I decided to drive her home.

'Let's roll the windows down and enjoy the night drive with cool air encircling us. I lowered the windows and it was indeed fun and I loved seeing Seema's hair ruffling in the fast wind caused by our car. She was engrossed in her own thoughts and I didn't feel like disturbing her.

Soon we reached her apartment and I bid her good night and drove off towards Bandra to get on the Sea link.

At the multi road signal at Linking Road junction, I stopped the car at the signal showing red. The signal is a long wait with at least a five minute wait. I was engrossed in listening to the Amar Prem album and I noticed the door opened of the car parked alongside mine and a burly Sardar come out and held my collar, meanwhile the other three occupants also came out and the sardarji shouted, 'I recognise you, you are the murderer of your friends wife, you madarc*od, come out.'

Another member put his hand in and opened the door and all pounced on me and started kicking and beating me.

'You fu*ker! You rape your friend's wife and then kill her and bury her in your backyard!'

I'm a strong man myself but to handle four drunks was beyond me and so there was nothing much I could do but to defend my head and lower part of my body. I could feel the pain of the kicks directed to my head and face. I heard the crack of my elbow and soon heard the siren of a police car and I remember telling the Cop to urgently take me to Hinduja speciality hospital at the inner road of 12th road Khar which was five minutes away and then I passed out.

I opened my eyes and felt myself covered in plasters and bandages with intravenous drugs racing through my veins, lying in the ICU.

'Who brought me here last night?' I asked the nurse attending to me.

'It was not yesterday but 4 days ago, you were in bad shape but God has been kind to you and spared your life even after doing such a sinful act. We were waiting for you to open your eyes so that your relatives could be informed.'

'I have no relatives who care whether I live or die.' Tears ran down the sides of my eyes and I once again appealed to God and thought loudly that what is the use of so much wealth you bestowed when I don't even have a single human being by my side and till date I've encountered only misery and nothing else.

'There is a young lady who claims she is your fiancée, the poor girl sits outside in the waiting hall morning and evening and once in a while we allow her to see you.' The nurse informed me.

'I don't want to see Amita, tell her to go away.' I requested the nurse.

'Her name is Seema and not Amita and she has deposited advance money for your treatment.'

Oh God, she must be feeling so hurt and guilty about allowing me to drop her home that night.

'Is the lady sitting outside, can I see her please?' I requested the nurse.

'I will let her see you for a few minutes. Later on, after the doctor has checked you, you will be shifted to the private Luxury room as officially applied by your fiancée. She will then be allowed to stay overnight if you want.' I ignored her last sentence and awaited her seeing me.

Soon, a curtain was rolled aside and I saw Seema in green antiseptic overall with a cloth cap and gloves on and she gave me a wide smile exposing her well formed white teeth but her face revealed extreme stress and lack of sleep.

'Hi dear Seema, you look like someone just came down from outer space.' I humoured her.

'You look like someone who survived an earthquake.' She chided at the counter attack.

'Seema, please check my trouser back pocket for my wallet and bring it to me.' She checked and brought me the wallet.

There were seven credit and debit cards and I made her write the code of each and then handed over my wallet and requested,

'Transfer into your bank Account the advance amount that you paid to the hospital and also pay the hospital another two lacs on account basis. Thank you for temporarily becoming my fiancée, otherwise they may not have treated me with so much care.' Seema blushed but kept quiet. Soon, the nurse arrived and escorted Seema out of the ICU.

'The doctor is on the way and will be taking the decision to shift you to a private room.'

At 4:00 PM, a team of doctors including a general physician, an Orthopedist and a neurosurgeon checked me in turn and finally gave clearance to have me shifted to a private room.

'Doctor, how long do you think I will be required to stay here?' I asked.

'Well there is a hairline fracture of the skull, thank God you escaped cerebral damage. Your two rib cages are damaged and your elbow has been dislocated including internal hemorrhagic at two places. It is suggested to keep you here for at least for 21 days.'

Late in the evening, inspector Rasheed Inamdar visited me and said,

'You are getting popular these days. You are again in the News. The day after the mishap you were projected as a villain, the blame was exclusively directed on you for drunken driving. I came to know about the full incident and sorted things out and had the four assailants arrested and put in judicial custody for attempted murder and also the matter was clarified to the press reporters.

'Thank you sir, I'm much obliged.' I spoke through a swollen and bandaged jawline.

'We are moving at a fast pace in your other matter and we soon hope to conclude whether you are a murderer or not. Get well soon.' The inspector walked out of the room. I wondered whether the get well was to see me in fit health or for my arrest.

I was shifted to a spacious room with an attached toilet and a 42 inch tv including a settee for a family member to sleep at night.

My stomach growled for food but doubted if I could eat with the bandage tied, for the time being my arteries were available for food intake. The nurse who was checking my BP heard the growl,

'It's a good sign that all is well in your stomach interior, perhaps tomorrow your face bandages may be removed.'

Once the nurse had left, Seema pulled a chair and sat close by and held my hand and gently massaged my palm and fingers.

'After you have recouped we will visit Vaishno Devi mandir in Katra, to have darshan and pray for your good health and rid you of all the misery that befall on you.' She comforted me.

'I wonder what evidence Inspector Rasheed has encountered for him to conclude what he said!'

'Let's hope and pray that it favours you, that is if you are innocent, as you claim.' Seema clarified.

THE INVESTIGATION

Chapter Nineteen

Fifty senior constables in civilian clothes sat in a conference hall and the meeting was conducted by Sub inspectors Pramod Pandey and Santosh Moghe. The crowd waited for the meeting to start.

Pandey detailed the murder case and eventually discussed the white Tempo carrier, along with the tracked route that concluded as the carrier passed under an overpass toward Jogeshwari West. Sub-inspector Moghe then assumed control and spoke into the microphone,

'We need to find this vehicle. The only help that I can give you is that the last two registration numbers of the carrier are 66, 68 or 88. We need you all to spread into all the lanes and sub lanes and look out for the above numbers. Even carriers of different numbers but with a white colour should also be observed. Pandey then resumed and said,

'It is to be noted that during the day the carriers are busy doing business and only during night after they have parked their vehicle for the night is when you have to move about at night and trace this vehicle. Day after tomorrow is Sunday, an ideal day to check. Any questions, you may ask now.'

A constable raised his hand and enquired, 'If we spot a suspicious vehicle, should we call you immediately, or are we supposed to take note of it and report to you later?'

'Good question. You are to report immediately and we will then decide on the course of action.' Pramod Pandey clarified.

'Your duty starts now and let me tell you that a sanction to use you all is only for five days and I definitely want results within this period, those who do not have their own motorcycles have been provided with one. Good luck!' The meeting was dismissed!

At sharp 7:00 PM, a posse of motorcyclists started from Malcolm Park Parsi colony and cruised into the veins of Jogeshwari West and at snail pace they moved, being vigilant. They were instructed to gradually move covering the areas and then proceed towards Goregaon direction.

In the first three days, the results were nil or were false alert. It is only on the 4th day, constable Bala Manik called sub inspector Pramod Pandey urgently, and both saw the number plates as 9466. Pandey removed a print of a CCTV footage from his pocket and compared the two number plates and there was no question or doubt about the last two letters matching.

Inspector Rasheed had just finished making love to his wife Mumtaz, he needed to be inside her and hold her tight before releasing the flood, giving him the feeling of the earth moving under him as if like an earthquake.

The phone rang and sub inspector pandey spoke, 'Sir we have found the vehicle.' Pandey waited for his boss to speak who was trying his best to get his breathing rhythm to normal.

'Pandey! Ask for a police jeep to pick me up in the next 20 minutes. He looked at the time on the wall clock that showed 11:00 pm. He had half a mind to delay and go early in the morning but Rasheed knew his responsibilities.

His wife heard the conversation and modestly holding her nightgown, she went to the cupboard and brought him a fresh set of clothes. The inspector wore them quickly and saying bye to his wife, he hurried out. Mumtaz was used to such emergencies, she wore her nightgown and went to bed praying to Allah for his safety.

At 1:00 am, Inspector Rasheed Inamdar was alongside the vehicle comparing the two number plates and he smiled at Pandey and shook his head in a positive affirmation.

'Shall we pay a visit to the driver pointing towards a small house painted green?' Pandey asked.

'Pandey and Moghe, the best course of action would be to wait till morning and then apprehend him and get him to the CBI quarters and then question him. If we make a ruckus over here, the whole neighbourhood will come to know and the guys who hired him will be forewarned.'

'You are right, sir. In the morning when the driver comes out dressed and ready, I will show him my badge and sit with him and get the vehicle to our station. Sir I suggest you go home and rest and me and Moghe will keep turning to stay awake. At 10:00 am, I will have the driver of the vehicle in your office.'

It is quite frustrating for policemen on vigilance duty to pass time, the long hours does have a toll on their mind and body. The wait is excruciating but he is duty bound which he accepts.

It was a great feeling to watch the dawn approaching and the stars above gradually vanishing.

Both the sub inspectors gave stale yawns and yearned to wash their mouth and indulge in drinking a hot cup of chai.

At 8:00 AM, a nearby tea stall opened for business and Pandey took the first turn to go to the tea stall. He splashed cold water on his face and with his right forefinger he rubbed his teeth and took a cup of tea and some biscuits and went over to relieve his colleague to do the same. Moghe returned and both relished the tea and biscuits.

At sharp 9:00 AM, the front door of the small green house opened and a frail man in his mid sixties wearing a kurta and pyjama with a white skull cap came out and inserted the keys to open the door of his vehicle.

Pandey went over to the man and said, 'Kyu mian, going to work?'

'Yes, I have to earn for the family,' The old driver asserted. Pandey showed him his police badge and instructed him to cooperate and proceed. Soon Moghe joined and sat next to Pandey.

'Saab what wrong have I done, at-least tell me that, I'm a poor God fearing man and have never done anything wrong in my life?' The old man pleaded.

'If you have not done anything wrong so why worry? We need to ask you certain questions and if we are satisfied then you can go.'

'Ya Allah!' the driver said to himself.

Soon the trio reached the CBI building and took the lift to the 3floor and sat on a bench opposite the inspector's office.

A few minutes later, Inspector Rasheed walked towards his office, the constable at his door gave a crisp salute and opened the door for the boss to enter. Within a few minutes, the trio were summoned in and after the customary salutes they sat and waited for the boss to talk.

'Salaam Walekum, Mian,' Rasheed spoke in Urdu.

'Walekum Salaam bhai jaan, why have I been brought here?' The old man politely asked.

'First of all, call me inspector Rasheed.'

'Okay inspector Rasheed saab, what have I done wrong? I have never done anything wrong in my life and now when my time is nearing to see the Almighty Allah, I have been accused of some wrongdoing, I beg to know what is my crime?' The old driver pleaded.

'What is the number of your vehicle?'

'9466, hazoor.' Inspector then removed a video clip of a CCTV which faintly showed the last two numbers 66.

'Are these numbers on your vehicle's number plate?' Inspector asked.

'Yes Inspector saab, there is no doubt. I know my vehicle very well.' The driver answered confidently.

'What is your name?'

'Amir Mohammad.'

Inspector Rasheed succinctly recounts the murder case of Mrs. Paro Singhal, providing details on the disposal of the body, which involves the transfer from the victim's apartment building to the accused's bungalow.

'Yes inspector I remember the case, I read it in the Urdu news and also heard it on tv, but why are you telling me, do you think I murdered the lady?' Amir Mohammad questioned with intensity.

'You are one of the culprits.' The inspector shouted and then spread all the black and white photos of the route that Amir's vehicle had passed through leading to the underpass from East to West.

'I want the names of the others involved or else I'm putting you in the lock up.' Rasheed threatens and waits for the other man to cough up.

'Allah kasam, I have no idea, I'm a simple God fearing man.' He folds his hands and pleads, 'Inspector saab, I'm a well respected man in my community in the area of my residence, my family reputation will be crushed in mud if anybody comes to know that I was summoned by the police or put in lock up. There is some misunderstanding saab, please give me a few days and scout around for some information.'

'Then you leave your vehicle over here and tell your neighbours that your vehicle is in the garage for repairs. I'm giving you just two days.' Inspector Rasheed threatened.

Amir Mohammad bent and gave a salute and started walking out. Suddenly he stopped in his path and after a moment of uncertainty, he returned to the table and said, 'Huzoor, I just remembered that about a month or maybe 45 days ago a strange incident occurred. I returned home after filling 20 litres of diesel which was a daily routine. The next day, I noticed that the fuel gauge showed the needle at reserve, I checked for any leakage and then I noticed mild grease sticking on the number plate, though it seemed all effort was done to completely wipe out the grease. Third, I noticed that there were traces of mud on the floor plate. I didn't bother about it and concluded that somebody had syphoned out the diesel for his own use and thereafter I forgot about the incident, until now that I remember.'

'Mian, are you telling us now to divert our attention?'

'No saab, I retain the filling slips to calculate diesel expense for the full year. I will check and show you the diesel slip where I took diesel in the evening and then filled it again the next morning.'

'Okay take a photograph of the two slips and share it on my WhatsApp.' The inspector gave his mobile number.'

Once the door was shut, the three looked at each other with some satisfaction at the progress they had made.

'I think the old man is telling the truth and since he has been a resident of that area for many years, he will help us to lead to the contract killers who stole his vehicle. I am keeping my fingers crossed.'.

During lunchtime, Amir Mohammad entered his house, freshened himself and spread the prayer mattress. He prayed for ten minutes and then went to the interior room and sat down for his lunch.

The moment his wife laid the lunch, Amir lost his appetite to eat and went to lay down on his bed and convulsively started weeping. His unassuming wife approached with concern, inquiring about the source of his distress.

Amir told her everything that happened this morning, the poor lady just had no words to say except only able to attribute his misfortune to the malevolent influence of an evil eye.

'Begum I've just been given two days to solve the mystery, I'm not God nor I am in the police department, I don't know what to do.'

'Why don't You speak to a lawyer and take his opinion, they just cannot put you in jail. After all, there is a procedure.'

'Police can find any evidence, out of the blue,cook up a story and throw you in jail. Life will be peaceful so long you do not get into the clutches of the Police. They can be ruthless.' Amir warned his wife. Suddenly he sat up and went to the bathroom, splashed some water on his face, combed his hair and headed for the door.

'Where are you going in the middle of the afternoon, rest awhile and go in the evening?' His wife persisted.

'The only sensible and educated person in our family is my nephew Shaukat Ali Mohammad, he will guide me accordingly. His fabrication shop is nearby, I will wake him up even if he is resting now.' He left home in a hurry and turned left, walking 300 metres. He stopped at a fabrication shop with various mild steel bars, angles and thin steel plates strewn all around with two or three men doing some welding work.

One of the workmen recognised Amir and went to the door leading into the house and soon Shaukat Ali came out and greeted,

'Salaam walekum, chacha jaan, please come in.' The nephew invited his uncle.

The uncle surveyed his surroundings with an apprehensive expression, and Shaukat discerned that something was indeed amiss. Leading him to the final room, which happened to be Shaukat's private space, he seated his uncle. Offering a glass of water and allowing a few moments to pass, he finally spoke,

'Chachu, you seem to have seen a ghost, please relax and tell me your problem.'

Little did Shaukat realise that he would be seeing a bigger ghost very soon.

'A month ago, my vehicle was stolen and brought back before dawn and I forgot about the matter. I dismissed the incident, considering it a prank orchestrated by some youngsters.'

'But Chachu, such matters must be reported to the police, did you report?' Shaukat asked.

'No I didn't.' Amir Chachu admitted.

'If your vehicle was used in a nefarious act, the police will investigate and may come to your door steps. I suggest that you report this matter to the police station and file an FIR against unknown culprits.' Shaukat insisted.

'But beta, the police came to my house this morning and ordered me to drive my vehicle and follow their police jeep which eventually reached the CBI building.'

'Really? Oh no! It must be some very serious crime that the matter is in their hands. What happened then?' Shaukat asked.

Amir chacha then mentioned all that happened in the morning meeting with inspector Rasheed Inamdar, dropping the bombshell at his nephew.

'My vehicle was used for carrying a dead body from near Ruia Park at Juhu and to the murderer's house near the main

Juhu beach. My number plate is visible on CCTV all along the road. You remember that terrible case wherein a youth murders the wife of his friend and buried her in his backyard. They have confiscated my vehicle and given me two days to find out the contract killers. Obviously they think the murderers must be in close proximity to my house to plan taking my vehicle.'

Amir suddenly realised that some health emergency had befallen on Shaukat because the blood had completely drained from Shaukat's face or he saw a ghost.

'Chachu jaan, now you go home and I'll meet you in the evening after Namaz.'

Shaukat shut the door to his room from inside. He spread his prayer mat and prayed, asking the Almighty to give him strength to think sanely and help him in his endeavour to safely ride the tsunami. He had never let himself get astray in any inter communal arguments, he treated all as equal and continued to run the fabrication shop to the best of his ability.

His childhood friend Mukesh Singhal has ditched him, his request to settle scores with a creditor was eye wash, he wanted help for bigger things and like an idiot he gave the name of Akhtar Kazi Mohammad to Mukesh.

Shaukat did not realise the damage he had done to bring the two murderers together. He started envisaging that very soon his name will also crop up in the newspapers. Being soft at heart ,he contemplated suicide but being a religious man he was aware of the tenets of Allah and so could not do so and sent to Hell. In the eyes of God he was not a guilty man he had not taken part in any murder and God may forgive him. He decided to go along with his uncle and meet the inspector and explain everything to him..

Tears ran down his cheeks and soon he was fast asleep in the posture of a baby in its mother's womb. In his deceased mother's womb.

He woke up late in the evening, he freshened and went across to his father's house and spent time with him and after having had his dinner he returned home. He was not yet ready to sleep and so he opened the holy Quran and started reading certain chapters. Later, he changed clothes and lay in bed hoping to get some sleep. Sometime during the night he finally slept.

Next morning, Shaukat woke up early and phoned his uncle to be ready at 9 AM and that he will pick him up and both will go and pay a visit to Inspector Rasheed Inamdar.

'I do not have his number but have the mobile number of his assistant, sub inspector Pandey.'

'Then phone Pandey that we will be at the CBI office by 11:00 am and would like to meet inspector saab. We have some important information to share.'

The two of them entered the huge building and without waiting for the lift, the two of them took to the stairs and hurriedly climbed up to the 2nd floor. Before knocking, Amir asked his nephew to wait until he had regained his breath and then signalled Shaukat to knock on the door.

On hearing a loud 'Enter!', the two entered and came over to sub inspector Moghe's table. The room was big enough to accommodate 4 tables and sub inspector Moghe occupied the table nearest to the door.

The sub inspector signalled them to sit, he picked his phone and called his senior colleague and Pandey instructed him to bring along the two to the office of inspector Rasheed. The four of them went up the stairs to the 3rd floor and knocked. The constable on duty opened the door and made way for the four to enter. The inspector had his head deep into a file and after a minute or two he looked up and invited them to be seated.

The inspector looked at an educated young youth and raised his eyebrows.

'Good morning Sir! I'm Shaukat and I'm the nephew of Mr. Amir Mohammad and I'm here to talk a lot and unfold certain mysteries in the matter of the murder case of Mrs. Paro Singhal.'

'What is your line of work, Shaukat?' The inspector asked.

'Sir I run a small fabrication shop and I love it. Rasheed took an instant liking for this young man who spoke fluent English and knew his etiquette of not talking in Urdu to gain brownie points.

'Okay Shaukat, start talking, no lies please, I hate people who lie. I will also be recording all that you speak.' Rasheed kept his phone on the table.

'Sir, May I also record, I need to keep it for records and refer to it when needed.'

'Smart man, you may record it.' Rasheed appreciated.

Shaukat started talking of his school days and his friendship with Mukesh Singhal and their continuous interaction by visiting each other's house especially on Sundays. The friendship continued even during their college days, though they studied in different colleges.

He spoke of many happy instances and later came to the day when Mukesh visited his house and mentioned that he is having some trouble with one of his creditors and if he can help him by introducing him to an anti-social 'dada' to threaten this creditor guy and get him off his back.

Assuming it to be a petty matter, Shaukat took him to the house of Akhtar Kazi Mohammad, a small-time local goon and he categorically mentioned to Mukesh to deal with Kazi directly and not to involve him in any further discussion. Shaukat further said that he never for a moment thought that Kazi had now graduated to doing bigger crimes. Shaukat stopped talking and looked at the inspector.

'Go on talk, you haven't finished yet.' The Inspector prodded.

'Later, after about 15 days, that is after the bad weather days, I read the news about the murder of Paro. My profound sorrow for the admirable lady was overwhelming, and I, admittedly, placed my trust in the narrative spun by both the newspapers and the police. Please excuse my candidness, but I found myself cursing Mukesh's friend for committing the murder.. In fact I went to his residence to console him.' Shaukat paused.

'Take your time, I appreciate your dilemma.' The inspector said with concern to Shaukat and looked at his two subordinates and an unspoken message went through the three that they were nearing the conclusion of the murder case.

'It was just yesterday afternoon, my uncle over here came to my residence and narrated about the sub inspectors visiting him and confronting him about the number plates and the journey of the vehicle from the apartment building of Mukesh. I may still not have doubted had the vehicle been stolen from some far off area. In fact, I am still not sure whether the small time goon whom I introduced to Mukesh is actually behind Paro's murder. That job is yours sir and if it turns out true then I'm going to be in serious trouble.' He starts crying and for the first time he speaks in Urdu and pleads to Almighty Allah with raised hands and questioning Him why he had been chosen for this despicable act. Amir chacha consoles his nephew and said,

'I am also in trouble and we need to prove that we had no hand in this murder case. Have faith in God.'

'The only way that you can be absolved is by disclosing us the address of the goon who I think was contracted by Mukesh to murder Mrs. Paro, furthermore he should declare that you and your uncle had no part in the ghastly murder otherwise you both may stand accessory to the murder and that can ruin your life,' Inspectors Rasheed cautioned them, though it was not intended.

Sometimes, inspectors must weave a tapestry of confusion, not just for those innocent of the crime but occasionally for the police themselves. Amidst the chaos, within the labyrinth of uncertainty, the truth silently orchestrates its grand reveal, awaiting the moment when clarity will pierce through the intricate veil of deception.

191

Chapter Twentieth

A gentle knock, and there enters Seema into my hospital room, carrying a variety of flowers. She carefully places their stems in a vase near my table.

'There was no need for flowers, your presence brings life to the room.' She pretended not to have heard me.

'How are you feeling?'

'Much better than yesterday and if you keep coming everyday, then I should be out of the hospital much earlier than the tentative date.' I prodded her again.

'The work at my clinic is going nice and fast and will be ready for business within a month. Also while I'm idling and watching the workmen at work, my thoughts stray in your direction.' She took a pause and continued, 'I have come up with a brilliant idea about utilisation of your Juhu bungalow. You had mentioned that the plot size is 1200 sq.Metres, that is a pretty big land to build a five star hotel of at least 10 or12 storeys and imagine all the floors above 5th storey will have a direct sea view, isn't it great?'

'Why do you think good about me Seema, you neither allow me to hold your hand, nor you express your sentiments? Why are you doing this to me, what are your intentions, I'm truly confused?'

'You men can never understand a woman's mind. Am I mad coming here daily just to see how you are feeling, I'm concerned about you that's why, but I cannot let my emotions run wild. I have faith in my judgement as a professional head Shrinker of you being innocent but there is always an iota of doubt which withholds me from maybe surmised as an encounter with a murderer, please don't misunderstand me, try to understand my dilemma.' Seema spoke softly and looked at me expectantly for my reaction and I shook my head indicating that I understood and agreed with her.

I moved my head away from her so that she does not see the tears running on the side of my eye and wetting the pillow. For the umpteenth time, I questioned God for putting me in such a serious problem and when things were getting bad, he brought solace in the form of Seema.

I felt the face towel used by her to wipe my tears and caressing my face through the towel,

'All will be well!' that is all she said.

'I have to go now, there's so much to do, I'll see you tomorrow.' she didn't touch me while leaving.

My thoughts went to my case matter and I suddenly remembered that the next date of hearing was on 28th of this month and since it was a criminal matter I'm bound to be present in court or else a NBW, (non bailable warrant) is issued onto me and the police is required to arrest me and produced in court for the next hearing. I definitely could not ignore the date.

'My phone buzzed, the heavy based voice of inspector Rasheed Inamdar was at the other end, I wondered if telepathy did exist.

'Hello Mahavir, how are you doing?' There was no sympathy in his voice.

'Getting better sir, some bandages have been removed though the plaster on my elbow will take another 10 days but overall I'm improving.' I waited for the reason for his call.

'Just to remind you that your date in court is on 28th and you must be present for the hearing. Judges take it seriously on absentees and I need to tell you to be well dressed with a light formal jacket over your shirt.'

'I will do that provided my elbow is free and the bandages removed from my head, otherwise I may have to take a certificate from the doctor and postpone the hearing.' I said.

'I've already spoken to the doctors and they are confident that you'll be okay and free to leave the hospital by the 23rd.' The inspector switched off.

I wondered why the inspector phoned, reminding me if the date is acceptable but guiding me on what to wear is something that I couldn't fathom, I decided to forget about it and hope for the best.

My thoughts took a circle and returned back to Seema. Her beautiful face appeared before me and I wondered why beautiful girls were attracted to me. There were plenty of good looking men but I suppose physical attraction is not all that a woman craves, it's the trustworthy appearance and facial expressions that attracts them. I was aware of one aspect of myself: both men and women were naturally drawn to me, seeking a connection in human relationships. Mukesh Singhal exploited these innate qualities, ultimately causing chaos in my life. As the consequences of Mukesh Singhal's actions unfolded, I found myself grappling with the fallout of misplaced trust and the intricate web of deceit. Little did I know, this chapter of my life would be etched with lessons about discernment and resilience, leaving an indelible mark on the narrative of my journey.

Chapter Twenty One

It was decided that Shaukat would walk past the house of the dreaded goon Akhtar Kazi Mohammad and when abreast the house, he would casually drop a ball of paper in that direction indicating the particular house.

Shaukat can then keep walking and further on take a rickshaw and go home. His work was then over. Sub-inspector Pandey and Moghe, donning plain clothes, led the way, discreetly trailed by half a dozen trusted constables, also undercover, at a short distance behind.

The two sub inspectors freed their pistols from the leather holster and placed it in their pocket ready to pull out in quick motion.

The duo watched Shaukat throw a ball of paper along the ground in the direction of a single storey house and continued walking casually.

The police contingent abruptly stopped and let a couple of minutes pass before they start walking and on reaching the house, they signal the six police constables to surround the house while Pandey and Moghe walk towards the door of the house and knock.

The door opened and a youth in a skull cap opened the door partially and stuck out his head and said, 'Who are you and what do you want?'

'We are friends of Mukesh Singhal and have brought an assignment for Kazi Saab.'

The youth went in with the message and nearly five minutes passed and still Kazi did not appear.

Kazi must have smelt a rat or he may have phoned Mukesh or else he may have seen them from behind the curtain and the goons are trained to recognise a policeman. Kazi may have been prompted by either reason to contemplate escaping and making a run for his life through the back door, unaware that the house was already surrounded.

Kazi pulled out his pistol and fired at one of the policemen and tried to run. On hearing the shot, Pandey ran out and as Kazi was igniting a motorcycle, he shot Kazi onto his leg who left the bike and while limping tried to run from the scene and soon enough he was overpowered by policemen in plain clothes. Sub inspector Moghe came over and kicked him hard in his guts, a couple of times and shouted, 'Mad*rchod you fired at a policeman, wait till you reach the police station, you bh*nchod.'

Kazi was a huge man but a bullet injury can bring agony to the strongest.

On instructions from Inspector Rasheed, Kazi was taken to a hospital close by and his bullet wound inspected. Fortunately the bullet had passed through and through the calf muscle barely escaping the shin bone. The wound was treated and stitched up and a pain killer injected and handcuffs tied on his wrist with the arms on his back.

'You bastard! You are lucky that your pistol shot escaped the policeman otherwise you would have been dead by now!'

The next few days, the police waited in patience for the bullet wound to heal, doctors stuffed him with antibiotics and other related medicines for quick recovery.

On the 10th day, Kazi was escorted to the interrogation room and subjected to questions and accusations about the killing of Paro Singhal. The goon did not budge and then he was mercilessly thrashed causing internal pain but still Kazi did not succumb. The beating continued for three straight days until he became unconscious but with a splash of water on his face, Kazi was brought to life.

Inspector Rasheed then took over. He presented himself as a figure as huge as Kazi and questioned him who stayed adamant. After an hour or so inspectors Rasheed shouted to summon sub inspector Pandey. Inspector Rasheed took Pandey to the furthest corner and said just loud enough for the words to be audible and instructed, 'This goonda now needs only one action and that is encounter killing, get rid of him. I want him dead by this evening, there is no other alternative.' The inspector walked out of the room.

Pandey called for Moghe and once again whispered but loud enough for Kazi to hear,

'Moghe! Arrange for two unlicensed pistols and as per instructions of the boss, we have to carry out his orders this evening.'

Moghe walked over to Kazi and asked,'What would you like to eat? What is your favourite dish? Hyderabadi biryani, mutton keema with parathas or gosht nalli with Kerala parathas, the choice for any particular dish will be served to you for today's lunch.'

Kazi then broke down and asked to meet inspector Rasheed. Pandey pulled out his mobile and phoned his boss and told him.

'Why have you called me, be quick, I'm a busy man and for the sake of Allah speak the truth, I'm warning you that if you lie I will ensure a dog's death to you.' The inspector threatened that while pulling out his phone and putting his device on recording mode, he made Kazi sit on the opposite chair and said 'start talking, you are informed that what you speak is recorded.

'I was hired by Mukesh Singhal.' Kazi stopped talking and looked at inspector Rasheed Inamdar.

'I heard you, keep on talking.' Inspector Inamdar said casually, though at heart he was excited.

Kazi narrated all that took place, how Mukesh Singhal approached him and how the deal was done. He further narrated about the fateful night when Paro Singhal was sent on a pretext to fetch some documents from the car and the moment she approached the car, he and his men strangled Paro Singhal.

'What are the names of your accomplices?' The inspector queried. Kazi blurted out the names and disclosed where they reside. The inspector gave instructions to Pandey to send a team and round up the other four guys. Pandey left the scene to comply with the instructions of his boss.

Kazi then spoke about stealing the vehicle and transporting the body to the bungalow including all that happened at the backyard of Mahavir. More questions were asked and Kazi answered them all.

'Kazi, it's a good thing that you confessed all. When the time comes for judgement, this act of confession will be considered by the honourable judge.'

'Take him back to his cell. When his four accomplices are rounded and brought here, make sure you inform me.' The inspector ordered Moghe and walked out of the room.

Chapter Twenty Two

While leisurely flipping through the newspaper at home, my phone suddenly buzzed—it was Seema. I straightened up and greeted her, 'Hello Seema, it's always a pleasure to hear your voice. What's the reason for the early morning call?' Unfazed by my affectionate tone, as usual, she proceeded with her conversation.

'Today is the 28th, your day in court,' she uttered, maintaining a thoughtful silence.

'I'm aware and the hearing is post lunch so I'm killing time, I'm cool my dear, and things will happen as destined.'

'I'm coming to your house, in fact I'm in the escalator, open the door and yes we will go to court together and that is if it's okay with you.'

'Sure you must come with me to give me moral support by holding my hand.' I went over to the door and opened just as the lift reached my floor.

She rushed into my arms and held me tightly and then released me and walked inside my apartment. I was overwhelmed with her gesture and followed her in.

'Have you had your breakfast?' She asked

'Not yet, the maid should be coming any moment, you'll join me? I asked.

'Today I'll cook breakfast for you, what eggs do you prefer, fried, omelette or boiled?'

She went into the kitchen and I guided her to whatever she required and helped her to prepare by toasting the bread slices. After a long time, I felt good in life. Seema's presence made me forget all my worries for the time being.

We sat on the table and ate a nice and fluffy cheese omelette with mildly fried tomatoes and canned red beans and finally washed it down with freshly brewed coffee. She bit into a buttered toast and having eaten it she finally said, 'Today is your court hearing and I'm going with you, you don't mind I hope so.' Seema looked up to me. My eyes watered, I looked the other way. There was no one other than her who was concerned about me. My parents, my brothers, and sisters treated me as inconsequential, and I had no friends. While acknowledging my potential faults, I couldn't help but wonder why I never engaged in arguments with anyone. I never envied another person, generally I was a courteous person so why people distanced from me. I mentioned to Seema all that came in my mind and asked her as to what could be the reason.

'Because you are a very fine man and everyone realises that they cannot match your humane qualities, so the fault lies with others and not you and let me tell you today that inspector Rasheed did not oppose your bail because he is also a humane and he gave you the benefit of doubt, above all your grandparent's blessings will always help you out of troubles.' Seema spoke with philosophical conviction. I did get some solace. I once again felt like holding her and intensely felt like kissing her but then I was always held back from displaying my emotions. It had to happen on her terms and I had to wait patiently, or will it ever happen, I wondered.

'Shall I put some music on for you while I shower and get dressed? The court hearing is at 2:00 pm so I need to be ready and moving at 11.30.'

I took a cold water shower and later vigorously rubbed my body dry, combed my thick hair growth. I chose to wear a light blue shirt with grey trousers and finally wore a Navy blue linen formal jacket. With a final appraisal in the mirror, I entered the living room and waited for Seema to put down the magazine and look towards me.

'My my you look dandy and may I ask why the formal attire?' I could see a twinkle in her eyes, inwardly appreciating.

I went towards a small makeshift temple with our deity's portraits in wooden frames, I lit an incense stick and prayed to God asking for nothing but their blessings. When I opened my eyes, I saw Seema standing by my side and praying. What surprised me was that while her eyes were shut, tears were running down her cheeks, her inner grief swelled out.

'Please Seema, you are my strength and if you break down, what will happen to me?. I sort of pleaded.' She immediately wiped her face and without looking at me, she said,'Lets go my dear Mahavir.' She smiled and headed for the door.

Chapter Twenty Three

The court was unusually full, probably expecting a revocation of Mahavir's bail. There were spectators whose only interest was curiosity, there were a number of junior lawyers and paralegal who attended to listen to senior advocates argue cases, there were a platoon of press reporters, some with hidden devices to capture the proceedings on video, there were also litigants waiting for their case to be heard. There was also Mr. Mukesh Singhal sitting in the last row as a co-respondent with his advocate sitting in the well for lawyers for this hearing. Inspector Inamdar and his two assistants stood by the side of the entrance in police uniform.

'ALL RISE,' the bailiff commanded, a side door opened, and a senior judge entered, signalling everyone to be seated. The Court clerk read out the case number and Mahavir's advocate Vandana Malik signalled him to proceed and stand in the accused enclosure, Mahavir disengaged his fingers from Seema's hand and entered the enclosure.

The prosecutor bowed to the judge and taking a deep breath he said,

'My Lord, there are some interesting developments that have taken place in the past 30 days.'

Suddenly, there was commotion at the entrance door. A huge man followed by four others with their hands cuffed were escorted into the room. All of a sudden, Mukesh Singhal got up from his seat and hurried towards the door. Four plain clothes policemen blocked the door and handcuffed Mukesh Singhal and dragged him abreast of Kazi and his henchmen. Pandemonium broke out in the courtroom until the judge rapped his gavel and silenced everyone and instructed the Prosecutor to speak.

'My lord, inspector Rasheed and his police team pursued the investigation and finally caught the Kazi gang who committed the heinous crime of murdering by strangling Mrs. Paro Singhal contracted by Mr. Mukesh Singhal, the husband of the victim, executed the crime. Kazi and the gang have confessed to the crime. In view of these developments the prosecution hereby wishes to withdraw the case against Mr. Mahavir Batra as he is innocent and instead file a case against Mukesh Singhal and others. On behalf of the Police department, we apologise to Mr. Mahavir Batra for wrongfully being accused in this case and we plea to you my Lord to set him free and instead allow all the accused to be jailed and criminal proceedings initiated against them.' With an audible sigh the Prosecutor sat down.

Once again the court hall erupted with reporters rushing out and contacting their immediate boss about the latest development, nobody was interested to hang around the court, the court hall was now nearly empty while various legal technicalities were discussed.

After an hour, when Mahavir walked out of the court building, he faced a dozen TV channel vans with the cameramen klicking his pictures on video and snapping.

They crowded around him, questions coming from all sides. While he answered a few, one question lingered the most: 'Who is this beautiful girl with you?' He simply replied, 'You will know soon.' Seema and Mahavir sat in the BMW and Ramesh the driver whisked them away from the crowd.

'Ramesh take me home.' Mahavir instructed his driver in a tired voice.

Rasheed Inamdar was back home early with a plastic bag filled with slices of Surmai fish, king prawns and Bombay duck, a thin watery fish popular on the Konkan coast, a real delicacy if prepared well. Being born and brought up along the coastline, he preferred fish to red meat. He had earlier phoned his wife not to prepare any dish for dinner as he was returning home with fish . His two children Saleem and Razia anxiously waited for him and while his wife cooked, he joined the kids to play Ludo and later watch cartoons.

At 9:00 pm, he switched to Maharashtra regional news channel and the main focus was on the Singhal trial. He soon shifted the channel to avoid the kids watching unpleasant matters.

After dinner, the kids were sent to their room to freshen up and get in bed.

While his wife Mumtaz sorted out the kitchen, Rasheed put on the tv and watched himself on the screen answering questions which were more specific to Mahavir and not answering questions related to Mukesh Singhal since the case was sub-judicial. His wife entered the room, and Rasheed switched off the TV, lying in bed. Mumtaz also lay there, her skin cool to the touch, emanating the scent of soap.

Tonight, he was in extra mood and prolonged the foreplay considerably until a severe urge erupted to enter her. Mumtaz was equally aroused and crossed her legs around her husband's waist pushing him harder into her. Their bodies slapped together until the rhythm escalated and a cry of fulfilment kept their mouth in a lasting kiss.

Later on regaining their breath, his wife placed her head on his shoulder and gently massaging his chest, she said to her husband,

'Now tell me the good news that you have been waiting to tell me.'

'You remember, I mentioned about a case where this man is accused of murdering his friend's wife and you had said that it seems the accused is falsely implicated?'

'Yes I remember, so what of it?'

'You were right. We have caught the real accused and this guy is set free.' He realised his wife was fast asleep, he smiled, shut his eyes and was also fast asleep within moments.

Chapter Twenty Four

Mahavir inserted the key and opened the door to his apartment, he made way for Seema to enter and then shut the door.

Seema came into his arms and they kissed, with their mouths sealed to each other. He effortlessly carried her to the huge four seater leather sofa and artfully got rid of his jacket and lay next to her on the wide sofa, for the first time he moved his palms on her beautiful face. He felt her delicate throat, moved his hands on her shoulder through her T-shirt, she shivered and they disengaged.

'This was my first kiss ever and it gave me a feeling of oneness.' Seema disclosed shyly.

'That's because you didn't find the right man, come let me give you more of it.' They kissed and kissed and suddenly Seema felt a teardrop falling on her cheek and then she felt Mahavir's body shaking in spasms.

'What's happened, my love?' She wiped the tears off his face with her palm.

'Seema I love you tremendously, you were the only person in this world who had faith in me, but for you I may have perhaps committed suicide, it does seem weakness but any person in my place would see a bleak future. You became the purpose of my life.'

They continued kissing and Mahavir placed his hand on her right breast and kneaded it. He felt her legs open and he lay between them and made her feel his maleness.

Mahavir restrained himself and promised to have a proper wedding night, it won't be proper to take advantage of her sentiments. He disengaged and saw Seema covering her eyes with her hand.

'Tomorrow is Sunday and since your dad will be home, I intend to come over to your place and ask your parents for your hand in marriage. My darling, I want to marry you and live with you all my life. We'll have lots of children and I'll make sure to make you a happy wife.'

'But you have not yet proposed to me, honey.'

'Will you marry me Seema Bhatnagar?'

'When did I say I will not, I love you and will surely marry you and now I'm famished and ready to eat at a full restaurant and while waiting for food please put on the tv.'

The News showed Mahavir looking extraordinarily handsome in formal clothes.

'Now do you realise why inspector Rasheed told you to dress up well. Because he had faith in himself and was convinced that you were innocent and that is why he did not object to your bail.'

With the arrival of the food, an unspoken dance of care unfolded as they served each other, their actions whispering promises of a shared future. In that intimate moment, emotions of understanding and affection painted the air, setting the stage for a journey where love and partnership would intertwine seamlessly, shaping the chapters of their life together.

THE END